A COLD PLACE IN HELL

A COLD PLACE IN HELL

WILLIAM BLINN

PINNACLE BOOKS

Kensington Publishing Corp.

www.kensingtonbooks.com

PINNACLE BOOKS are published by

Kensington Publishing Corp.
119 West 40th Street
New York, NY 10018

All Kensington titles, imprints, and distributed lines are available at special quantity discounts for bulk purchases for sales promotions, premiums, fund-raising, educational, or institutional use. Special book excerpts or customized printings can also be created to fit specific needs. For details, write or phone the office of the Kensington special sales manager: Kensington Publishing Corp., 119 West 40th Street, New York, NY 10018, attn: Special Sales Department; phone 1-800-221-2647.

PINNACLE BOOKS and the Pinnacle logo are Reg. U.S. Pat. & TM Off.

ISBN-13: 978-0-7860-2076-8
ISBN-10: 0-7860-2076-8

First printing: July 2009

10 9 8 7 6 5 4 3 2 1

Printed in the United States of America

I

There was a bunch who said that what Billy Piper did that Fourth of July was dumb, but it wasn't dumb, because Billy Piper was not a dumb cowboy. What he was, truth to tell, was a *young* cowboy, and while there are those who say that means the same thing, saying it does not make it so. Billy was just young and intent on impressing Pearline, and that is the reason why he put his hand up and said he could ride Black Iodine right into the ground.

It was Independence Day, which you knew, but that was not the reason for all the ribbons and hoorah. Fourth of July in Salt Springs, Wyoming, is also the wedding birthday for Mr. and Mrs. Fergus Blackthorne, and Fergus, being richer than buttered sugar, has always hosted a town party to celebrate that fact. You might see Mr. Blackthorne and wonder why he felt the need, but that wouldn't be none of your concern. Mr.

Blackthorne always said he gave up his independence on Independence Day. He said it every damned year he threw one of these things, and there'd be tons of people to laugh because we all lusted for free whiskey and beef, both of which were plentiful in all directions.

Billy Piper isn't Gospel sure, but he thinks he was seventeen or eighteen on this Fourth of July. Not that his age is an item that matters much. What matters is what happened after he took Fergus Blackthorne up on his bet that no one could stay on Black Iodine for more than ten seconds, which did take a sackful to make the bet, when you knew that no one ever stayed on Black Iodine for seven seconds, much less any Go-to-Hell ten. But Billy wanted to impress Pearline and she wanted to be impressed, just the same.

Pearline worked as one of the girls at Honey's, and she was Billy's girl. Not that Billy was the only cowboy she took upstairs for stroke and poke, but there was other stuff going on, even times when he'd go to Honey's and she and Billy would just sit out on the airing deck of her room and watch the sky and talk. Honey hated that and the example it set, but Billy, just a rider for the Starett ranch, couldn't afford to be at Honey's more than two times a month, so the sky-watching times didn't cut into her profits much more than a mouse bite or two. So when a time like the Blackthornes' Fourth of July came around, and Billy and Pearline could just walk out like they was Pastor Smith and store clerk Jones, no one much minded that going on. They both had a lot of tough swear times in the normal part of their lives, so no one blamed them much, no one wished them sour.

Everybody started to cheer when they brought Black Iodine on out of the barn. They had his head all wrapped in burlap to hold him in check, but it didn't seem to be all that good at calming him down. He was still fractious as they get, tugging this way and that when they brought him close to the rail where Billy Piper was waiting to climb on.

"It's going to be all right, isn't it, Wilbur?"

I looked over and there was Pearline standing next to me. She had a lacy hanky in both hands, all balled up like a cat's toy. There was nothing but tremble in her smile. "If there's a man can do it, Billy's the man," I said. She didn't believe me and neither did I. She was porcelain with pink cheeks, and I wished I could have said something better than I did.

Billy's backside hit on Black Iodine and away they went, dust kicking all around with the crowd screaming and Pearline chewing on that balled-up lacy hanky. Seemed to go on forever, but of course that's not true. Later on, the timer said it was about a whisker past six seconds when that hellcat sumbitch reared up and frog-flipped back, coming down with Billy Piper flat under him, screaming like you don't ever want to hear a man scream, or anything else, for that matter. Maws was covering kids' eyes and tugging them away, while cowboys come pouring over the top rail; Fergus Blackthorne one of the first, me a couple of puffs behind Fergus himself. There was hats waving and men pushing on Iodine's flank, trying to roll that bastard horse off Billy, who had stopped screaming, stopped moving. I could hear Pearline yelling out from the other side of the fence, calling out his name over and over. Other girls from Honey's was trying to pull her away, but Black Iodine turned her man into muddy blood. When Black Iodine finally rolled away and bucked up to all fours, I saw Fergus's skinny hand go to his holster and wrap around the butt of the hogsleg there, thumbing back the hammer while he pulled it free of the leather.

I clamped down hard on his wrist. "Don't do it, Mr. Blackthorne. Billy wouldn't want something like that done. He wouldn't want it, sir!"

Fergus Blackthorne looked at me the way dogs look at you when you try to stop them from humping your leg. Mr. Fergus was a substantial man in town, wasn't used to taking orders from an old Texas waddie like me. He chewed on what I said for a time, then let the hogsleg fall back into the holster. "You're right," he said. "We'll let Billy do it when the time's right." And we both looked back over at Billy.

They got a blanket under him and was lifting him, four men to a side. He made a noise, a spittle noise, but he didn't know it. The eyes were closed tight. His left leg was turned in a bunch of ways legs don't turn. The pants leg was soaked clean through, dark and hot.

They started walking off with Billy, moving in the direction of the barn, and I could hear people calling out for Omar Jordan, who wasn't a doctor but was as close as we had in Salt Springs, being as he spent thirty odd years in the horse soldiers and had seen pretty much every kind of gutshot and shatterbone you could see, and if he wasn't a doctor, at least he'd been there for times when a real doctor had to be around and might remember what got done. I didn't want to see what was going to get done to Billy. His bottom half looked like matchsticks on the trestle after The Special passed, and I didn't want to see any of it at all. I took me a step in the direction of Rooney's Rest, and this time it was Fergus Blackthorne's turn to do some wrist clamping.

"You're his pard," Fergus said. "Be good if you're there when he comes out of it."

"If he comes out of it."

"Be good if you're there either way."

Which was true right down to the ground, and I knew it. Still, I wriggled once more: "He won't know if I'm there."

Fergus's hand had picked up a liking for folding around the butt of that pistol of his. "Wilbur, you got me to show mercy to that damned horse a few seconds ago. I'm not a man who's known for showing mercy twice in one day."

"You wouldn't shoot me."

"I'd feel bad, that much is true. But I've always felt bad before. It doesn't last long." The look in his eyes would have to warm up a lot before you'd call it cold.

I turned away and started for the barn to see whether Hell was going to claim Billy Piper full-time or just rent him out for a spell.

II

There were sun spears shooting in through the cracks in the barn wall when I pulled open the door and edged my way in. They had Billy on an old door resting between two sawhorses. I was sorry I let Fergus buffalo me into coming here. It smelled of horseshit and piss and bad cheese. And there was the sounds coming from Billy, swamp sounds and gut-groans. Somebody shoved on past me and I saw it was Omar, and the wobble in his walk made it pretty sure they located him at the oak altar rail in Rooney's. There was a bunch of men clustered round the door table where they had Billy, and they all parted when they saw it was Omar who had come in.

Them parting like that gave me my first good look at Billy, and there wasn't anything good about it. They'd stripped off his britches and what was there was awful. Pink baby skin and red dripping meat and muscle, with snow-colored bony parts jaggering through at various parts. Billy and me sometimes'd go bony-butt raw in Bear Creek, so I knew his left leg had a knee about halfway down, but you couldn't prove that by what I was looking at now. If you cut the strings on a puppet, the legs might end up like Billy's left one was now.

"Dear dark Jesus," Omar said when he walked around the door table. Then he made one more circle and said it again: "Dear dark Jesus."

"Omar, tell us what to do."

"Be easier if he was a horse. We'd be done in no time."

"He don't look like a horse to any of us, Omar. Tell us what we need to do."

Omar rubbed his face. It was all rolled wrinkles. Pie dough like a young girl'd make first time out. "Have some of the women tear sheets up in strips about this wide, then boil the strips till they're too hot to pick up. Somebody else go find six, eight straight stout branches. Like you'd use for a cane. Three feet long, say. Take a knife, slice away the offshoots. Bring 'em here." Omar looked over the circle round Billy. He stopped looking when he fastened on a no-chest bald buzzard at the far end. Willard Ganeel. Store clerk. "Willard, there any laudanum out to your place?"

"You know there is, Omar. My grandpa's got the growth."

"Needs it, does he?"

"Fierce."

Omar nodded down in the direction of Billy

on the door table. "Then leave some for your grandpa, Willard, but bring the rest on out here to this boy, because I'm about to put him through a Hell the Devil thinks is a lot too harsh."

Willard Ganeel did not move for a number of ticks, looking from Omar down to Billy, then back up to Omar a final time, before he wheeled around and left the circle, popping on his derby hat just before he shoved the door open and got into the sunlight. One by one, we all moved off from the door table, finding some shade in the corners, hunkering down, not saying a thing as there was not a thing to say. There was just the waiting to do, and none of us were very good at that. Wyoming doesn't breed that in.

Door opened and we all started to get up, thinking the hot sheet strips were coming in or the straight tree limbs. (We all had our doubts about the laudanum.) But it wasn't any of that. It was Mr. Starett. He never showed his face at the Fergus Blackthorne Fourth of July hoorahs because him and Fergus were skunk and housecat both wanting the same spot of sun under the tree. They both had considerable money, but Mr. Starett also had considerable courtly concern that he brought with him wherever he had cause to go. Not that Fergus Blackthorne didn't have his own style. He did. Shit probably has a taste, too.

Mr. Starett walked slow to where Billy Piper was put. He stared hard. His mouth was tight. "Is he dead?"

"He wasn't that lucky, Mr. Starett."

Starett looked over at Omar, not liking what he just heard. "Can you fix him, Omar?"

"I can try." He knew that sounded empty. "I will try."

"Will he be able to cowboy again?"

"No, sir. Don't look for that. He might be able to set a horse, ride a little, but he'll never get it back to hell-bent, Mr. Starett. Never be doing that again." Omar cleared his throat. "That's all on the bet I don't kill him while I'm trying to fix him."

"That could happen?"

"Could. Pain can do that. It can kill."

Starett's hand reached out and his fingers touched Billy's cheek. Billy didn't react, didn't budge. Starett talked without looking away from Billy's face. "Wilbur Moss? You in here?"

"Over here, Mr. Starett."

"You can stay with Billy."

"Cookie's looking for me to help out, sir."

"I'll deal with Cookie. You stay with Billy. You sleep here. You eat here. You're Billy's chum. Now he's your job."

I didn't want to step up to the line and tell Mr. Starett the only reason I was in the barn there at all was because Fergus Blackthorne kicked my ass in there, not because I was all that tight with Billy. Though, come down to it, I was, and that was why I didn't want to go in, because he was a pard, a chum, and didn't laugh at me and my ways like some of the other boys did. "Whatever you want, Mr. Starett," was what I said, what I settled on.

The sheets came in still steaming, carried in a wood laundry tub.

Right behind came Matthew Brodbeck with the stout limbs, which were more straight than not straight. Omar sent two men out to the trough to get a couple of buckets of mud, though he didn't say what he needed mud for and if he'd had told us, we still wouldn't have done anything but go out and get those buckets of mud. Omar told me to go out to the Starett place and get what I'd need to stay here and when I asked for how long, just said "long," and I accepted that just like we went along with the order to get buckets of mud. When I was just going on out the door, in came Willard Ganeel. He was carrying a glass jar, filled almost to the top with something copper-colored. We nodded to each other. He headed for Omar. I headed for the sunlight.

There was a circle bench around one of the oak trees outside the corral fence, and that's where Pearline was waiting, along with two other girls from Honey's. There was Arlene, who said she was from New Orleans and might have even been telling the truth, and the other was Rosalie, who was nice enough, pretty enough, but coughed too much for my peace and was always emptying spit into the hankies she kept close. I went over and sat down next to Pearline, keeping distance from Rosalie.

"Is he awake?"

Shook my head. "And won't be for a time. Omar's filling him up with laudanum to knock him out while they're doing what they can."

"Will it hurt?"

"I expect so, Pearline. What happened to him is bad." Rosalie cleared her throat, brought a hanky to her mouth. There was pink on the hanky. I edged back around a little in Pearline's direction, took her by the hand. Her eyes were satin soft. "Pearline, Billy won't be the same after this is over with. Don't know how bad it's all going to be when it gets to the other side of things, but won't a piece of it be good or easy."

There were some soft little pops way off in the distance, off in the direction of Gundersen's pasture. Fireworks. Fourth of July. I'd almost forgot.

Arlene reached over, tugged on Pearline's sleeve. "Time for us to get back, Pearline. Honey says there'll be a stampede after the barbeque."

"Arlene, I can't be there today. Not after this. You tell Honey. She'll understand."

"Hell she will, Pearline."

Just then, there came a scream from inside the barn, louder than the fireworks, loud enough to make the horses tethered to the corral top rail rear up and try to pull away.

So much for Willard Ganeel's lawdmandamn.

III

"Wilbur?"

Someone was calling me. Somebody old, somebody with a whiskey voice, a cigar growl, the sound of pure spittoon stink. Wasn't the kind of voice you'd want to wake up to. Wasn't the kind of voice that ever said anything made the room better for it being said.

"Wilbur?"

I opened my eyes the way you'd pull off a poultice. Crisscross slats way up high above me. Sunshine coming in steep from the side. Eastern light. Sunrise. I was in Fergus Blackthorne's barn. It was Billy Piper talking to me.

They'd put the door flat on the floor so he couldn't roll off in the night. There were flannel ties wrapped around him, waist and chest. His left leg was stiff with dried caked mud, the straight stout limbs were under that, all layered with the sheets that had dried up stiff around his leg. I came up on one elbow. "Hey, pard . . ."

He cleared his throat a couple of times. I scrambled over and grabbed on to the canteen. Wet his lips. He took in what he could and cleared his throat once more. He had his regular voice back when we talked, but spiderweb, not solid. "What the hell happened to me, Wilbur?"

He didn't remember a solitary thing after climbing up on the fence when they started leading Black Iodine over in his direction. I told him what I could best as I could, making it sound like he'd stayed on Black Iodine a little while longer than he actually had, and just said he got his leg bad twisted under the horse when they went down. Didn't mention the screaming, the maws pulling the kids away.

"Lemme see," Billy said. "Lift me up. Lemme see."

I got an arm under his shoulders and lifted him up a few inches.

He looked at his left leg for a long time, studying the way you'd study a first-time river crossing. He looked, closed his eyes, looked again.

"Got me a leg like a sidewinder," he said.

"Does it hurt?"

"Throbs. Hammer-hammer-hammer." He let his head fall back. There were drops of sweat all over his forehead. His breathing was deep and slow, like he was trying to keep it slow, hanging on to hold level. "Who did me? Omar?"

"Omar, yeah."

"He say when I can get up and around?"

"Nope."

"He say *if* I'm getting up and around?"

"Nope. You want some more water?" Billy nodded and I lifted his head again, brought the canteen to him. He took a long pull of it. When he put his head down, he closed his eyes tight, real tight, and I remembered that Billy was still just a kid, no matter how much swagger and sweat he gave off.

"I'm going to ride drag the rest of my life if I can ride at all. That's it, isn't it, Wilbur?"

"Seems to be. You want some more water?" I knew he just had some, but it was all I could think of to do.

"And if I can't ride at all, Wilbur? What about then? What's there for me to do around here if I can't sit a horse anymore? And don't offer me anymore goddamned water. I've had plenty of goddamned water, all right? And it's the worst damned water I ever had in my life anyway!" The last couple of words his voice got louder and louder, higher and higher. I didn't want to see Billy Piper cry. More deep breaths. He covered his eyes with an arm. "Throbs. Throbs like a son-ofabitch."

"Sorry."

"And I asked you a question. What can I do around here if I can't sit a horse anymore?"

"I didn't answer the question, Billy, and that ought to be answer enough."

Don't know how long we just stayed there like that, Billy with an arm covering his eyes, me standing there next to him, not having anything to say that wouldn't hurt him more, and him having been hurt already more than a man ought to be at his age. Both of us might still be just like that till even now if we both hadn't heard that piping little ocarina bird singing its way to us from outside the barn.

If it was an ocarina, and it was, that meant Pearline had sent little Nicholas over to check up on Billy. Nicholas was the little colored boy Honey kept around to sweep out behind the bar and run the towels upstairs. And times when Yancy had to leave off the piano to go and use the outback privy, she'd let Nicholas sit on top the piano and play his ocarina, which didn't fill up the room like Yancy's piano, but it filled in the times when there wasn't anyone talking, and places like Honey's don't thrive when there's bunches of silence. Smoke and whiskey, cackling laughter coupled with stroke 'n' poke, that's what Honey's was made of. And Nicholas had a sunshine of a smile and the doves all liked him and looked after him, pushing him off to one side when too much bourbon turned the bulls into bullies and cheroot smoke and gun smoke started to dance together. Nicholas had a roof.

Nicholas had food. There's worse ways to stay on top of the grass.

"Hey, Billy Piper." Nicholas poked his head around the corner of the door. The ocarina was in one hand. In the other was a take-along can from Rooney's. "Pearline sent me to Mr. Rooney's for you. I got biscuits and blond gravy here."

"Sounds good, Nicholas. Come ahead." Billy moved up on one elbow. It was more movement than I'd seen out of him since it all happened.

That gravy smell reached me and Billy about five seconds before Nicholas actually got to us. Damned fine smell. First time I saw Billy smile since it happened, too. Would done Pearline a world of good to see that smile.

"You want a plate of this, Nicholas?"

"No, sir. Pearline sent it over for you."

"And you plan on telling her if you had a helpin'?"

Nicholas allowed that a little thought. He looked at Billy. Big round eyes, puppy eyes. "Reckon not."

They only had two plates with the take-along tin, so that gave me a chance to act generous and excuse me, head over to Rooney's for my own order of biscuits, with the chance of adding a glass of beer in there to make it the perfect breakfast I was hoping for. Billy understood, and I said I'd be back before a little bit and headed on out the door. There wasn't any talk behind me when I left, just the two of them blowin' the hot off and slurping it down as fast as they were able. Pair of raccoons woulda had more manners.

My foot just hit the bottom steps of Rooney's porch when Mr. Starett called out to me. He was at his table at the big bay window, which was open, just finishing off his plate of steak and onions. "Wilbur! You comin' on in here?"

"Yes, sir."

"Be quick about it. I'll buy."

That last part always makes me quick and so I was. When I pushed in through the door, I could hear Nicholas and his sweet potato piping in some little melody. Didn't recognize the tune, so maybe it was one of the kind he made up himself and played for Billy and Pearline on the airing deck at Honey's. Hoped so. That'd help Billy's mood some. I'd never seen Mr. Starett take a sip of anything that wasn't water or coffee, so I didn't order any beer with my biscuits. No point in having him think he had a barleycorn buzzard on his spread.

"You see Billy?"

"Just come from there."

"How bad's the hurt?"

"The leg-hurt, or the other?"

"Both."

"The leg-hurt throbs, he says. He can't talk much about the other."

Mr. Starett tossed his napkin down on the table, looked out the window to the street. Across the way, ol' Ganeel was sweeping out the boardwalk in front of the store. The morning sun come in low, shooting through the balloon of dust, turning it golden, cauliflower you could see through. "What the dickens are we going to do with Billy, Wilbur?"

The "we" part let me know I just got a new job.

Mr. Starett went on, still looking out onto the street. "I talked to Omar last night. He sent a wire to the Army surgeon at Fort Laramie. Surgeon said he'd try to get out this way next week or the week after, but he told Omar that if Omar was talking true about what Billy's leg looked like when we cut away the pants, that the surgeon's first thought woulda been to lop the damned thing off above the knee."

"Lord God. That'd kill Billy, Mr. Starett."

Starett nodded. "If the loppin' off didn't kill him, the sight of him being one boot too many might have done the trick once he woke up. Omar says Billy's never goin' to walk right. He's going to look like a top just running out of spin." He rubbed his face. Early in the day, but Mr. Starett was a weary, weary man. "How old's Billy, Wilbur?"

"Seventeen. Eighteen. Something like."

"Sonofabitch."

"Yes, sir."

Tolliver arrived with my biscuits and gravy, but I wasn't hungry anymore. The beer would have helped some.

* * *

The next four weeks was like reading a book that had the same thing written on every page. Omar and me would wrap the leg all over again, tighter if we could, and take off the dried-up clay and repack with new. Billy did what he could to stay quiet and not yell out, and was more times than not able to do it, though he sweated through his shirt most every time we went through it. The surgeon from Fort Laramie got there after a couple of weeks, and gave us a schedule about when we should start trying to get Billy up on his feet and get him to walking as best as he was going to be able to do that. He was pleased about Billy's leg and toes staying pink, and got us to arrange for Pearline to come over twice a week and squeeze up and down on Billy's leg. Called it some kind of massage, and I could pretty much see the kind of massage Billy thought he was getting.

"I ain't been with Pearline in more'n a month, Wilbur. And she starts squeezing on me like the Laramie major says and I get breathing deep, but I know I can't do anything with Pearline while my leg's like this on account of my not being able to move around like a man wants to move around when he gets rooster-y."

"Maybe there's another way."

"Another way to what?"

"Maybe you don't have to be in the saddle, Billy. Maybe there's a way for you to be the horse." The look he gave me was the kind of look you see on a dog's face when someone gives it an order in a language it never heard before. It wants like everything to obey; it just don't know how. "You think Pearline knows about this rooster-y thing goin' on?"

"Wilbur, the person we are discussing is my Pearline, who earns daily bread at Honey's house. Of course she knows."

"You talked with her about it?"

Billy shook his head, little-kid-like. "A man doesn't talk about rooster-y matters, Wilbur."

"She might know a way to help."

"You think?"

"More like, I wonder. More like, she can't know how to help if she doesn't know you need help."

"She knows. I told you that. She knows." He got himself a little feather of a smile. "I'm the only one she lets kiss her on the mouth. I ever tell you that?"

"No, but I sort of puzzled that out on my own."

"I'm the only one she lets kiss her on the mouth," he said again. "All the boots get parked under that bed, I'm the only one."

"You're a lucky man."

He looked down to his clayed-over leg. Didn't say anything. But looked. Looked hard.

"Shame you won't ever be able to put your own boots under there ever again," I said.

His look stayed hard, but now it was on me, not the crooked leg. "Talk it plain, Wilbur."

"Pearline's room is up on the second floor.

Man can't get himself to the second floor if a man won't get himself up and walking."

"You think I'm ready?"

"I don't think anybody knows, not me, not you, till we shove a crutch up under the arm on your rank side and see just what Black Iodine left you to work with."

"Don't seem like he left much."

"No, not much at all seems like."

Billy tossed back the flannel cover and looked at his legs. He lifted the bad one an inch or two, then let it lower on back. "My one leg's skinnier than the other, all leathery-like."

"I see it."

"Bird's wing, more than a leg."

"I see it."

Kept on looking at the leg for a long time, then finally cocked his head up and put his eye on me again. "Wilbur, tell me this. When you expect to get started on that crutch?"

Twenty years back, I was riding drag in Texas for the Rydell bunch when the horse I was on went and died, right under, just a couple little wheezing rattles; then he went down, first in front, then the rear, rolling over and over, pinning me under like you'd pin a flower on a dead man's lapel. I shoved and wriggled and called the dumb sonofabitch a dumb sonofabitch, but it was pointless, when you take into account the dumb sonofabitch was a dead dumb sonofabitch. The herd was in front of me, the boys looking the other way, so it was a time before any of them knew I wasn't where I was supposed to be and came on back to get me. I don't know how long it took them to get back, but it was enough time for flies to get to the dead dumb sonofabitch holding me down there in the loam, enough time for those goddamned feathered dead-flesh-eaters to start circling high above. The time it took for the boys to get back to me didn't seem as long to me as the time it took to get Billy Piper off the floor of Fergus Blackthorne's barn.

Wasn't for want of trying on Billy's part. There was plenty of that. But there was even more pain than there was trying, and the first time me and Omar rolled Billy up onto his feet and got him to put weight on the crunched leg, Billy didn't make a sound, not a mumbling word, but what he did was just faint away, and would have gone all the way to the floor if Omar and I wasn't there grabbing him hard.

It was Omar saw the good part to it, that Billy, even when he was going out, had turned himself so he'd be falling on his back and could stick his bad leg straight out from the fall. Wouldn't be making it any worse than it already was. We splashed some water on Billy's face, and he opened his eyes a couple of seconds after that. He looked up at us, then over to the crutch still tight under his arm.

"I went down?"

"Like an old termite tree in a windstorm."

He nodded, took in a few deep breaths, looking up to the ceiling. He held up a hand. "Get me up. Let's do it again."

"You sure?" Omar said.

Billy fixed him hard. "Omar, I like you. You helped me when I needed more help than I ever dreamed of. I hope you live sixty, seventy, eighty, a hundred years. And if you do, I promise you, you will never ask a stupider question than the one you just asked. Now help me get my rump off this little floor and let's get after doing it again."

So that's what we did.

Every day at sunup, once coffee got drunk and innards got emptied, Omar and me would work with Billy, shuffling him this way and that around the barn, looking like we were helping Marvin Whelper out of Rooney's at the end of a Saturday night. By the time we finished, Billy's shirt was black and sopping, his skin was mother-of-pearl pale, and he had knees made out of melting butter. From time to time, Nicholas would show up with a tin of foaming beer, sent there by Pearline, who wanted to know how Billy was coming along, but didn't have the deep gut it would take to stand aside and watch him go through what he had to go through. When it was done, Nicholas would play on that sweet potato of his, and Billy would lie back and sort of shake until he either got it all in line again or actually drifted off and was asleep. And that sleeping brought around another situation that made it all upside-down cake and that was Billy was sleeping when he ought to be awake, meaning he was awake when he ought to be asleep. Him and Pearline didn't see as much of each other on account of that, him sleeping at the only time of day when Pearline could leave Honey's to come see him. Sometimes, I get back from lunch at Rooney's and find Pearline just sitting there, holding his hand, patting his forehead dry. Didn't like to see that. Reminded me too much of a lady at a grave.

But it did seem to both me and Omar that Billy was making it better on his barn walks, even with the problems of sleeping and waking wrong. One night, after about four weeks of trundling Billy around, I woke up with a privy need and was relieved to see Billy sound asleep. I decided to give myself some more relief in the outback house and left him there on the barn floor, breathing deep, stopped just this side of a full-bore snore. I sat there in the outhouse for a time, mulling over things important to a cowboy who don't bounce in the saddle the way he used to, who knows that Mr. Starett's got an admirable heart, considering how he was treating Billy, but that he can't keep that many declawed kittens in his kennel. My back hurt and my eyes were more fuzzed up than I liked to let on, and all I seemed to hear late at night was a clock ticking away, louder and louder and louder. Especially in the middle of the night sitting in an odor-rot privy. Once my business was finished, I yanked up my drawers and went back outside. You forget how good fresh air can smell until your own stink gives it a hammer hold. The sky was sprayed with stars and it looked to be a clear day to come. The moon was just a sliver, a smile of white against a black blanket. I went back inside the barn.

Billy Piper wasn't there.

The flannel was all rumpled up, and there was a scrape of scuffle marks in the dirt beside it. Then the scuffle marks trailed off and I saw a boot print. Next to that was a long smooth place, and there was a circle-dot right next to the smooth place. Another boot print and the same things next to it, pointing off in the direction of the double door leading out to the corral. And then I knew what I was seeing. Boot print. Foot drag. Crutch dot. Boot print. Foot drag. Crutch dot. Boot print. Foot drag. Crutch dot. Billy Piper had gotten himself up and was off and moving.

The steps and the drags was easy to see in the moonlight. They went straight across the corral to the gate and out then into the street. If he'd'a gone on the boardwalk, I wouldn't know which way was which, but he stayed straight down the middle of the street, moving out around a couple of the muddy patches, but straight on still, past Rooney's and the store where Willard

Ganeel clerked, and it wasn't till I saw the trail curve around the corner that it come to me and I knew where Billy was headed. He was going in the direction of Honey's and Pearline. And just when that set in solid on me, I saw them coming out of Honey's front door. There wasn't a light on in Honey's. There wasn't a light on anywhere except from the sky, but there they were, walking out like it was Sunday after singing and they were Mr. and Mrs. Kissmyass.

Pearline had on a white nightdress. There was a light blue shawl thing around her shoulders. They moved slow, Billy dragging the stiff leg like an anchor. She walked on the other side, holding on close to his arm. If Honey had looked out the window and seen one of her favorite girls walking out in the middle of the night, she'd a thrown a shoe and then a fit.

I could hear Billy and Pearline talking, but their voices were low and the words were all knotted around one another. I sulked back into the shadow side of Rooney's and tried to stay as still as I could. They wouldn't want me to hear them and I didn't really want to hear them, but they were still talking whispers and coming closer to me and Rooney's, so staying in the shadows seemed like the only fair thing I could do.

"If I can't walk, I can't ride, and if I—"

"You're walking fine."

"Like a possum flies."

"It'll get better the more you do it."

He stopped, shaking his head. It hadn't been easy, this trip. He was breathing deep. "Might be, but I'll tell you this. I'm never going to be able to cowboy no more."

"Mr. Starett likes you, Billy. I'll bet he could find a way for you to work with Cookie."

Another head shake. Quick. No give about it. "Wilbur Moss is Cookie's helper. I couldn't step in to that place. Couldn't, shouldn't, won't."

"You'll find something."

Billy turned to her. He put his free hand on her cheek. "I already have," he said. And then, just like he said was so, he gave Pearline a kiss on the mouth, there in the empty three-in-the-morning street all filled up with moonlight. Then Pearline said something soft. Billy nodded a bit, then swung around, heading back in the direction of Blackthorne's corral and barn. Pearline stood there watching him scuffle off down the street. She lifted her hands, covering her chin and lips, just watching him. Then she turned away herself and headed back toward Honey's. Her hands were balled up tight.

Slow as Billy was moving, it wasn't hard, even for a bony runt like me, to get back to the barn before him. I scuttled down Swede Alley, behind Rooney's, then cut over and come in the barn the back way. I was just pulling up my blanket and bedroll when I heard Billy get to the front door of the barn and pull it open. I closed my eyes and rolled up tight, figuring to look asleep.

Heard every step, every foot drag while he came closer. He let the crutch just fall, then teetered himself forward, breaking his fall with his hands, keeping the game leg out stiff behind him, then flipping over so he could lie down on his back. He groaned, a no-more sound, then breathed in deep through his mouth. Pretty soon, his breathing slowed up and I thought he might be at rest.

Then he said: "Wilbur." Soft. "Wilbur?"

I didn't move. Tried to be fake asleep.

"I walked all the way down to Rooney's tonight." He waited for me to say something, but I was afraid to, afraid I'd say something that would tell him I was watching him and Pearline. "Seems to me it's time to talk with Mr. Starett, see what he's got in mind."

I stayed quiet. Somewhere way in the distance, I could make out Nicholas playing his sweet potato, a little piping birdsong.

"Night, Wilbur."

I still acted asleep, and pretty soon I actually was, so for all I know, little Nicholas played that sweet potato all the way to the dawn.

I never had kids, which is probably a good thing for those kids I didn't have, but walking with Billy that next afternoon on our way over to talk with Mr. Starett, I started to get a whiff of what it must be like. It was easier for Billy to walk in the street than on the boardwalk; too many steps on the boardwalk and they were hard on getting up and down, but walking in the street

made him and me look like a two-man parade.
And as we went, there were people coming out
of the stores, calling out.

"Hey, Billy! Look at you!"

"Who's that walkin' there? That Billy Piper?
Who'da thought that?"

"Billy Piper! Land's sake! Good on you, Billy!"

Omar came out front of Rooney's, lifting
a schooner of beer in our direction. Willard
Ganeel stood in the doorway of the General
Store, making that little "o" thing with his thumb
and index finger. Well intentioned, but looked
silly. And there was girls in the windows at
Honey's, lacy camisole things, all smiling, some
blowing kisses. Pearline was there, and her smile
was smaller, but not less happy. And Billy waved
and smiled back. Touched the brim of his hat.
Even seemed to walk a little more spry. And I just
sniffed that whiff of what it must be like to be a
parent. Felt like a good thing. Little scary, a
lot good.

Rooney's was the only place I ever saw had
shinier floors than what was in the entry hall of
Mr. Starett's house. I'd never been inside his
place before and when I glanced over at Billy, his
bug-eyed look while he was looking around told
me I wasn't the only first-timer standing there.
There was a big painting on the wall by the stairs,
picture of a handsome woman in her forties

or so, green velvet dress, hair all circled up at the back of her head. Her eyes were wide, dark, ready to bolt out of the frame if you looked at her too hard. That'd be Mrs. Starett, who wasn't here anymore. Not that she was dead, she wasn't, but the winters and the bone chill took those dark eyes to a place without a downspout. She was somewhere back East now and Mr. Starett never talked about her, but he always thanked you when you asked after her. She might not have been in the house anymore, but she was still in a place close by as far as Mr. Starett was concerned.

He took me and Billy into the back office, and I admit I was trembling inside. It's one thing for Billy to be brave and generous when he's got Pearline's perfume all around, but I wasn't totally certain what he might say if Mr. Starett was to offer him a job working with Cookie, putting my bony butt back onto a saddle and riding dusty dirty drag for the rest of my days. Fact is, it's a pretty quick idea to get to and one that stands pretty tall and strong. I could have saved myself the lick-lipping nerves. Mr. Starett covered my bet.

There was a map spread out on his big desk, each corner held down by a shotgun shell. He rapped a knuckle on a circle he'd made on the map. "Here's where you're going, Billy."

We both leaned forward and looked down to

the circled part. Then we looked at each other. He didn't know; I didn't know.

"Mr. Starett, I don't know what I'm looking at, sir."

"You're looking at the timberline shack on Jupiter View. You're looking at the place we lost about forty head last year. You're looking at the cabin at timberline on Jupiter View where you're going to spend all of next winter."

Billy said, "I see," but that was a lie, and Billy's look shouted that, so Mr. Starett went on.

"I've got Heflin and Benboy up there now, putting up firewood and filling in the chinks. Once they're done with that, they'll put the corral back where it ought to be. Once they're done, the place will be a castle. Well, no, no, not that. But it'll stand up for the winter, and that's what you'll need."

Billy's voice was reed thin. "Mr. Starett, I'm not about to take any charity. That's not my way."

"Me neither. This isn't charity, Billy. You think I'd be sending Heflin and Benboy up to do all that work on the maybe you'd go along with this? Uh-uh. Somebody's going to be up there this winter, Billy. Somebody's going to make sure I don't lose me another thirty, forty head. I'd like it to be you. I think it's a job you can do for me. No cut riding, no hopping around. But if you don't want to do it, then so be it. But there's going to be somebody up there this winter, Billy. Somebody's going to be getting those wages, whether you give the say-so about yourself or not."

"And if I say no?"

Mr. Starett found a dead cigar in the dish next to the map and took it up, finding a match, firing it up with a thumbnail. It glowed as he puffed. Balloon of smoke from the other side of the desk. "Well, that's when we might start talking about that charity you're not so fond of."

Billy's head went down. He leaned on the desk.

Starett went on after a time for a time. Wouldn't send Billy on up till October, which would give him a couple months to work on the leg. How they'd teamster him up with weaponry and shells, food in cans and hardtack sacks, everything that they could think of to get him through the time up there. It was a plan and like it or not, there's always something to be said for a man who's got a plan.

"Gimme a day?" said Billy.

"Sure thing," Starett said. Then: "One way or another, Billy, I'm sending someone up there to winter it through and hold down the number of beeves I'm losing. Don't see why it shouldn't ought to be you."

We were done, but Billy didn't know how to get out of there, so I jumped on, thanking Mr. Starett, grabbing on to Billy's elbow, and tugged Billy back toward the door and out onto the shiny floor at the front door part.

Out on the porch, Billy took a count to settle

his hat right, get the crutch lined up under his arm. I offered him an arm when we started down the steps, but he didn't want that, which was no surprise.

"Ask you a question?" I said.

"You just did."

"Can you explain to me one good reason why you'd tell the man no? He's offering help, is all he's doing."

"I'd be away from Pearline four, five months, Wilbur."

We were at the street now. Turned back in the direction of Blackthorne's place. "Billy, you was too young for the war, but you know about what they call the conscription, don't you?"

"I do."

"And what would you call somebody who was so bothered because he'd be away from his sweetie for a long time and decided not to soldier with the others on account of that? What would you call him?"

"Wilbur, there was a war going on then. Different. Different all the way up, all the way down."

"Look at the dice, Billy. Count the dots. They count up plain as pus. You are in a war. You're in as much of a war as you're ever likely to be in, and if you've got a name to call on those boys who wiggled past conscription that you don't think you ought to call on yourself, why, I'll just shut up and listen because that's an explanation I don't want to miss."

We was all the way down to Rooney's before Billy spoke up. "How long'd that war last, Wilbur? How long were those boys off in the war?"

"A year. Sometimes longer."

"And when it was all done, the girls was still there waiting on them? None of them went off?"

"None's a hard word, Billy. Most stayed. Some might have gone through a hole in the fence. But I think you got to realize, Billy, it isn't like Pearline's goin' to a lot of church socials and selling box lunches for the cause."

I would have thought an eagle was trying to claim me; that's how hard Billy's hand clamped down on my shoulder. He turned me to look at him square on. "Wilbur, you're too old and bloody brittle and I'm too wobbly still, but if those things weren't the truth, I'd take that last remark as my permission to knock your head off to one side."

"I'm sorry I said it, Billy. True or not, it shouldn't have been said. You and me don't need to be hammering at each other."

He appeared to take that as a good answer. We walked on again. Heel boot. Foot drag. Over and over. Then, when we come around the corner to where we could see Blackthorne's barn, Billy said: "I'll tell Mr. Starett tomorrow."

"You taking him up on it?"

"I got a choice?"

"Not that I see."

"Me neither." I stopped us walking to the barn. "I got enough jingle to buy," I said.

"I got enough thirsty to drink."

We turned tail and went to Rooney's then.

That next day, we moved back into the Starett bunkhouse and things got put back more or less the way things were before Black Iodine frog-flipped on Billy. I went with Cookie each day out to Weemer's Pasture where Mr. Starett had a crew looking to see if the creek could be dammed up and turned into a watering pond.

Billy spent most of the afternoons in the tack room, mending and stitching as best he could, doing what he could to earn his keep. He'd be there for supper at nighttime, but when the arguments started or boys just went off moon-crazed, Billy just set out walking, crutch and all. He didn't like folks watching him struggle with the action, and he thought if he was out there after the sun left, he wouldn't be laughed at, wouldn't be felt sorry for. Saturdays, he'd ride into town, his own leg out stiff, looking like a K plopped down on horseback, and he'd be at Honey's, trying to gouge out a bit of time with Pearline, though that was hard on Saturday nights. That was hard on them both.

Then, something mysterious happened that no one involved could explain, even though it had happened to each and every one each and every year they'd been on the face of this earth.

Summer left the room and there was October standing in the door.

It was time to load Billy Piper up to the top of Jupiter View. Mr. Starett said it was Miz Starett who made up the list of what was to go in up the way with Billy. Mr. Starett had them put up the high sides on the supply rig, and when I saw what all Willard Ganeel had piled up on the General Store loading dock, I figured we better hitch up a couple buffalo to hump that wagon on up to the line shack. Didn't know what all Miz Starett thought Billy was going to need to get through the winter, but whatever the hell it was, she was making sure he was going to have it. Better to have it and not need it than need it and not have it; that must have been her way of thinking. Poor horses.

The plan was to take Billy up to Jupiter View that next Monday, and it took a couple granite-hard hints to Mr. Starett that a wage advance to Billy on the Sunday before might allow him a night's farewell with Pearline, who he wasn't going to see or talk to or touch for the next four months. Starett wasn't easy on the issue.

"If it was anything but to be used for him going over to Honey's, it might be a different matter, Wilbur, but my wife's a stern believer, and she definitely doesn't hold with paying for my boys to go over to Honey's and spend out."

"Mrs. Starett, she's Temperance, too, isn't she?" I said.

"She is."

I'd seen decanter bottles in Starett's house filled with honey-colored bourbon sniffing liquid, which made me comfortable with thinking the Temperance Pledge in that house had a lot to do with whether or not Mrs. Starett was on the property or not. "She know that some of the wages you pay are spent over on Rooney's bar?"

"I'm sure she might assume that's the case."

And I didn't say a mumbling word. Just stared at the man. Worms on the end of a hook been more at ease.

"'Course, it might be a rumor," he said.

"What's that, sir?"

"Man could go into Rooney's and have himself a cup of coffee, too. There's no rule about who orders what."

"Yes, sir."

"For all I know a man could go on into Honey's and just play pool."

"Or pay little Nicholas to play some favorite tunes on his little ocarina."

"That, too. Could pay little Nicholas for favorite tunes. I imagine a young man like Billy Piper might have a lot of favorite tunes."

"More than anyone could count, Mr. Starett."

Starett went to his desk and pulled out a black metal strongbox with a numbers lock. I turned away and looked out the bay window. Heard the sound of crinkly paper. Starett cleared his throat. I turned around. He shoved an envelope across the desk in my direction. "You tell Billy this is a going-away congratulations."

The envelope wasn't bulging, but there was enough congratulations in there to promise a pleasant Sunday night for Billy and Pearline.

The only thing we didn't take into consideration was Billy and Pearline. We put together a special hoopla for them both, but what got clear quick was that they didn't want to have us there, didn't want to hear the toasts and the hollering. They both smiled, but they was the kind of smiles that never showed teeth, the smile a ten-year-old saves for fat aunts on a hot day.

Once the message settled in on us, we looked over to the bar and the tables with poker chips, and that gave Billy and Pearline the chance to venture up the stairs and into her room. Honey even bought for everybody around then, which served to take attention off whatever was taking place in Pearline's room, whether it was reading posy poems to each other or Billy playing serious bed bounce like he was a stag in serious wide nostril rut. None of our business either way.

There was ground fog and breath frost all the while I gave Heflin a hand putting the team of dray horses into the harness. We was almost ready to go by the time Billy walked Whiskey, his old mare, on up to us. Didn't look as if he'd seen any sleep the night before, but it might have been he saw a whole lot of bed. His eyes got wide as doorknobs when he saw all the boxes and barrels in the back of the high-sider. He didn't know he'd need this much.

I mounted Geezer, and me and Billy fell in behind Heflin and the wagon. The sun was just nudging the night off to one side when we creaked down Main and pointed toward the foothills. The top of Jupiter View was all wrapped up in gray ribbons of clouds, like a woman in a storm. We were both hunched down, and the only noise was the wagon wheels and Heflin mumbling "sonofabitch" each time the wagon bounced on one of the ruts studding the road. Heflin's back was always a damn bastard, and this trip was not likely to make it a boil you'd want to kiss.

Time came it was light and even a little cooler the higher up the trail we got. It was narrow enough for me and Billy on Whiskey and Geezer. For Heflin and the wagon, it got to be a circus tightrope boiled in butter. Pretty soon, Heflin held up a hand, said he needed to stop and wring out his wrangle, though I think he was just bled dry by the road and all its switchbacking. Billy and me swung off the horses and just stood there puffing a bit. We could hear Heflin watering the aspen. Billy turned and looked back from the way we'd come up. Salt Springs was a clump of something hard to make out at the base of the mountain.

"It might be some kind of conjure," Billy said.

"What might be?"

"The farther off you get from things, the smaller they look. They don't seriously get any smaller, they just look like they do. Not sure why that happens. Not sure why. What do you think, Wilbur?"

"Best you say that again. Not so quick."

He pointed down the trail. "All those buildings look real small. But they're not real small. All those buildings are just the same size as when we rode out of town. How come you think that's the way of it?"

Out of the corner of my eye, I saw Heflin come waddle out of the road brush, buttoning up his front side. "Time to draw rein," I said to Billy. "Let's get to it." Billy didn't fuss about it, started moving right to Whiskey, but he backed to the horse, looking down the side of the mountain to Salt Springs every step of the way.

Heflin and his crew had done a good job at the line shack. They'd filled in the chinks with mud and leaf-mulch. There was enough firewood stacked high to melt most of the moon, and the little corral off to the back was built sturdy and high. The trees stood tall around the shack, but you didn't have to tilt your look much to see that part of the mountain that was rock and ruin. Inside, the place was buttoned down good. To most, it wasn't a big place, but to Billy, coming out of the bunkhouse he shared with twenty hawking, spitting, stinking, two-legged-hog humans, it musta looked like a palace.

We got Billy to walk around outside and look

things over, being as his leg made him helping pretty much an echo in the mud. So, me and Heflin unloaded the wagon. Then, he unpacked some of the boxes on one side, while I opened up some of the barrels on the other. We were up high, so there was more huffing than talking, though at one time he said: "That boy realize that trail's closed off after serious snow sets down?"

"He realizes."

"He realize no one's going to be able to get up here to check on him?"

"He realizes."

"No help coming if he takes a tumble and hurts himself?"

"Heflin, I talked with Billy Piper. From what he told me, he doesn't plan on falling." Nothing coming back from the other side of the shack, and I looked out to the corral. Billy was standing there at the gate, lifting the latch over and over, just using one hand, like he might have to do if he had a lead on a stray beaver and couldn't grab on with two. Just for a flicker, it crossed my thinking that Billy looked smaller to me because he was standing farther off than usual, but that kind of thinking can muddy up your milk if you're not careful.

There was only about three hours of sun left by the time we had done with the unloading, so there wasn't a liver left to play with. Heflin was out with his wagon and teams, tightening the leather, while Billy and me stood in the doorway of the shack. There was the two of us, and that meant there wasn't a person in that room who was easy with show-off farewells. I rubbed him on top of his head, and he told me to take it easy on Rooney's bottled rot, and we laughed at nothing in particular, so I rubbed on top of his head one more time and moved off to the wagon, after Heflin popped a whistle to get me moving.

I tied Geezer off at the back of the wagon and climbed up next to Heflin on the seat. The team leaned into the traces like they was eager, grateful not to have to heft on down what they just got through hauling on up. We bounced along for a minute or two before I switched cheeks and edged around to look back.

Billy was standing in the door of the shack, the light from the fire behind him, looking like he was cut out from the mountain air itself. Had one hand on the door frame, the other holding on to the crutch. He was all crookedy with his leg the way it was. If he was a doll, you'd tell your little girl there wasn't any way to put it right. Broken means broken for good. Bounced along in the wagon for a few ticks, still looking back, with Billy never moving out of the door, looking after like he was being his own carpenter, putting together a memory from scratch and for good.

He looked real small by the time we rounded the first downhill and couldn't see him anymore.

Mind: He wasn't really small; he just looked it.

IV

Nobody ever fell in love in the dead of spring. White weddings don't happen in the dead of summer. No perfect pink baby ever got born in the dead of the fall. No, it's the "dead" word and winter that dance together long time after the fiddler's gone home. I figure that's because the winter's a cold time and we know dead is the time when we're all going to be cold for the rest of forever.

And Salt Springs was in the dead of winter. It was a time we all turned into moths, scurrying from one warm light place to another, pulling ourselves in tight during the between times, goin' from Rooney's potbelly to Cookie's stove, rubbing our bottoms, wringing our hands quick against each other. The wind was a cold sound, a ghost call, and there wasn't anyone who wasn't looking for the thaw to come.

Some didn't last long enough to see it, and

went and got dead during the winter. I hated to hear of anyone dying in town, because Mr. Starett called himself a civil-minded man and it turned out to be our job, as his hands, to dig the graves, and Wyoming loam in the winter is what people call granite in other places. If any of us had had a heart burst while we was digging, the others would have just rolled the body in on top of the coffin goin' into the dark part. Waste not, want not, and no having to dig a second hole.

Sweetheart Mary Harper was the first dying we had, and you don't know her because nobody did, because she was only two days old when she turned as cold as the sheet ice on her family cabin roof. Her momma was Hannah and she was eighteen, though the look in her eyes when she was at the graveside was a whole lot older. One point, she looked away from the grave, up to the way-off mountains, capped white and hard, and I knew she had to be wondering why. Why me at this place, why me standing next to a baby didn't ever get the chance to see the sunshine or run through a meadow? Why me at this age in this godforsaken, goddamned place? Why Sweetheart Mary?

There wasn't any answer, of course, least not one Hannah could have heard. She couldn't know the place wasn't all that godforsaken, just a place where you had to be as tall as the cold mountains killing you, as deep as the black canyons and jaws squeezing the life out of your heart. If you could get that tall and go that deep, you might just find you were the climber for that hill. At least, it was a small grave me and young Thorpe had to dig.

Willard Ganeel's grampa was the next one to go, and it was a mercy that he was free of the growth. Night, Grampa. Rest now.

The next hole we had to dig was the hardest. It was the Coughing Girl at Honey's. Somebody snuck into the room, or so Honey said, and put a quick pillow over her face before he used the pillow to muffle the shot that sent a bullet through her brain. Whoever done it went out the window then, left it open, and when Nicholas went in to wake her the next morning, the blowing-in snow had covered her all up like a comforter. The blood soaked through the snow, like a red cherry into a milk puddle. Honey and all her girls were at the puttin'-in, standing there in their best, shivering, leaning in against each other birdlike. I didn't see a one of them cry. Their faces were stiff and set hard. Looked down into the hole but never at each other. I guess there was a lot of snow when the Coughing Girl got killed, on account of no one ever found footprints in the snow under the windowsill.

The final grave we dug was the one we least of all expected to, and that was the hole that got put aside for the wife of Fergus Blackthorne. They had gone to bed and when Fergus got himself awake the next morning, she was white and cold as the frost on the window. He went running out into the street in his nightshirt, wailing and crying loud for help, but Salt Springs didn't have any resurrectors living there, and Mrs. Fergus Blackthorne was going to be looking up at the underside in her very best dress. Everybody who came to see her before the planting said she looked just like she did in life, and I thought that was an uncommon cold thing to point out. Mr. and Mrs. Starett both come to the puttin'-in, but that's because Blackthorne and Starett pretty much run what running Salt Springs needs, and that's like being eyes at an ear party; you just naturally hang together and figure you know more.

What happened next wasn't about anyone dying, but I think it went more than a couple rods toward helping Salt Springs die. Most didn't hold with me. Most thought it was a fine thing when they discovered we was sitting on a pond-ful of oil under our very feet.

No one said it was oil at first. It was just this sliming slippery shine on top of the water on One Legged Indian Crick. It was one of Blackthorne's teamsters who had Texas time, and said he thought he'd seen it before and if he was seeing it again, then he said it was oil, dirty gold. Blackthorne and Starett had people come in from out of state to put a name to the slimy shining scum, and when they was done, oil was the name that fit. Which opened the shithouse door and sent word to all the out-of-state flies, so in they come.

The engineers and the railroad transit peepers, not to mention the tent city workers and the card-playing maggot poppers.

Rooney's started staying open twenty hours a day, and would have stayed open longer, but he needed the off time to restock and mop up the puke and tobacco juice. He covered up the mirror behind the bar and took down the naked lady pictures. No truth to the rumor the naked lady was Rooney's sister.

Honey's business picked up similar and the few times I saw Pearline, she had deep black rings under her eyes and didn't smile at all, though she hadn't smiled hardly a bit since the Coughing Girl got killed, now that I think of it. Her lips'd turn up like a skinny smiling moon, but it wasn't a smile that ever got to her brown eyes. She looked older and she looked more scared, which hardly ever goes together right.

There started to be talk that Salt Springs was going to have to have a city setup, a mayor or a council or both or something in between. There was talk about all the planning and backfill that needed doing, and I stayed out of all those talks. They pointed to puff-belly importance and complications, and I know enough about the West to know it's not a place that gives easy seed to complications. It only seems to make things fester and grow crooked, if they manage to grow at all. Strikes me that if the answer you got is complicated, then what you really got is just a whole new set of questions. There might be places where it's right, places where people get easy in that chair, but one of those places is damn well not Salt Springs. Not now. Not ever if they was to make Wilbur Moss king. That hasn't happened yet.

Not that there was any stopping what was going on; there wasn't. People were making plans and repainting signs, figuring on new people due to arrive who wouldn't know about Rooney's and Honey's and the livery and General Store and such. Struck me that if that was so, then we were expecting a whole parade of pretty dumb-betted people, but that happens when complications check in.

Important as the oil lure was, even it couldn't seem to stop the thaw from taking the stage, and Mr. Starett started to look up to the mountains, telling me it was close to time to get the high-side wagon and head on up to fetch Billy. We had to wait till the mud turned regular and would take the wheels, but I started to feel an itch to see him, find out how he got through all those long dark times and whether or not he thought out any plans for how he was going to keep his skinny butt full enough to keep his drawers from sliding to boot tops.

I couldn't know the answers to all them questions and that Billy Piper had changed even more than Salt Springs itself.

I give out with a whistle call when the high-side

got over the final rise and I got my first look at
the line shack since we left Billy standing in the
door six months back. The cabin looked pretty
much like I remembered it. Weathered a little bit
while winter was there, but the same thing was
true of Wilbur Moss, come down to that. Then I
saw Billy come out from behind the shack, and
what I saw let me know we were done with one
song and I didn't know the words of the one to
come. That was on account of the fact that Billy
was walking towards me and waving his hands
and smiling that sloppy puppy smile of his, and
doing all of that without any crutch being anywhere in sight.

He wasn't walking like you or me; he had to
kinda throw one hip out to the side and yank the
bad leg along after him, but if it wasn't walking
like you or me, it was still walking and the damned
crutch was stacked somewhere in some corner
and God bless it, likely to stay there.

The sloppy grin was the same as it used to be
before Black Iodine frog-flipped, and all I could
think of at first was how happy Pearline would be
to see that smile on her right-hand pillow. I drew
rein and Billy looked up at me from over the
rump of the back horse.

"Hey Wilbur," he said.

"Billy."

"I don't want you to get killed, Wilbur."

"It'd be good if we both knew what you were
talkin' about, Billy."

He tilted his head back, peered up at the sky, lifted a hand to shade his view. "Lots of gear to load in the wagon and the sun's slipping all the time and looks to me we might lose the sun halfway back down the road. That's hard driving, Wilbur, even for you. Don't want to see you get killed. Might be better to load on out and then spend the night. Leave in the morning."

He nodded. "That'd give us a chance to lighten the load going back to Salt Springs."

"How we goin' to lighten the load?"

Billy Piper's smile went from sloppy puppy to wolf cub. "We could get rid of the bourbon Mr. Starett sent up here with me. I'm about half a jug to the good on that, and I don't know if you know it or not, Wilbur, but unused bourbon is heavier than devil dung."

Him and me looked at each other for a time; then, I couldn't stop myself from laughing. Sonofabitchin' kid coulda sold fire to a dry forest. "Suppose you tell me where you'd like me to tie down this team a horses?"

So he did.

We were done with eating and the fire shadows were bouncing all over the ceiling. The jug was still making gurgling noises when we rocked it, so we took the time to sip and spit there in the night. Most of the talk was nonsense and lyin', but when the cold set in and the wind began its terrible dirge, it all got quieter between us, with the silences filling up the time more than before.

Like I remembered the look of Billy standing in the door when we drove off, he remembered the same time from his end of the time.

"Don't know how long I stood there after you and Heflin went down over the other side of the rise, but it was a considerable chunk. You know how the mountain is, and I could hear you going down the trail for a long while. The wheels, the horses snorting and snorfling. Even the reins creaking sometimes, so help me God. Even the reins. And then there was nothin'. Just the empty road, the wind, the creaking from the limbs and hawks crying out way high. I felt like I was dead but breathing.

"Went on into the cabin and started to uncrate what got brought up. Lots of tinned beef and some dodgers and biscuits that looked like rocks or rocks that looked like biscuits; I never could tell which. The one crate I already told you about, the one with the bourbon jugs."

"The last soldier of which we're killing now."

"That we are, anything to make it easier on the team going down."

"Poor horses."

"Makes their load lighter. We're both doing our part, Wilbur. A man's got a hard road to go, looking after the horses like we do." Billy reached over and got the jug, adding another layer of gold on the gold on his cup. "You want to help more, Wilbur?"

I took the jug. "Love those horses."

"Poor things."

We clinked. "To the horses." It warmed all the way down. "Least, Starett took care of you being stocked with what you needed."

"He did good. Mrs. Starett did better." He saw my look and stood up slow, wobbled a bit, then went to one of the crates shoved up against the far wall. His dragging leg made a draggy noise on the dirt. He put his glass on a shelf and lifted the top off the crate. His hand waved me on over.

I heaved me up and went over to stand next to him, looking down into the crate. What I saw went far to telling me why Heflin bitched and moaned about his back being ruptured out all the way on the ride back down to Salt Springs. The crate was stacked from one side to the other with books, red-spined, blue-spined, purple-spined, thick and thin and thumb-thick, most with yellow glitter printing, titles and writers and such, or so I figured. I laughed, coughing up a teaspoon of bourbon bile to the back of my throat. "What the hell was she thinkin'? What the hell she have in mind?"

"Don't know clean what she had in mind, but she saved my life, Wilbur. That woman saved my life."

He ran his hand over the backs of the books, the way you might pet a dog you loved that was sleeping by the fire; soft as stroking a soap bubble, don't want to wake the critter. He started to talk about his first days in the high mountain cabin, about the gray and the bone-deep cold, about how quick the dark came once the sun was behind the North Peak on Jupiter View. First coupla nights, he just bathed his brain in bourbon, he said, but he knew that was heading for a cliff, so he sliced back on that. And pretty soon, he started looking through that big crate that had tormented Heflin's back so bad.

"Didn't know you liked to read so much, Billy."

"I didn't. I could read store signs and wiggle my way through the chalkboard at Rooney's, but that was pretty much what it was. But up here it was just me and nothin', and the books were the only other somethin' there was."

So he read. Found one of the books was a schoolbook reader and he used that one a lot, so much that he started reading the real books, the ones with people and stories and big killings and such. He yanked one up and looked at it like it was an old friend. Billy opened it to the first page with all printing on it. He read out loud. "It was the best of times; it was the worst of times."

"Billy, that don't make no damned sense."

"Sure it does, Wilbur. Right down to the boot heel, it does."

I reached out for the jug. This road was turning in ways I didn't feel good about. "Tell me how that makes any sense."

He stared at the air for a second, then looked back at me. "Suppose you're pump-humping some sweet soft lady, and just as it happened that you were going to start to geyser in her, your heart exploded and you died. Wouldn't that be the-best-a-times-worst-a-times?"

"I don't know about that, Billy, but I know you just put a thought in my skull that's gonna make my next time at Honey's more interestin' than I'd like it to be." I looked at the crate. "You read all these damned things?"

"Most, but I couldn't get around the knitting books and the ones about baking pies. Miz Starett must love baking her pies."

"Or Mr. Starett likes pies and he keeps giving her books to nudge her into the light."

Billy smiled and nodded, then said something that made me think I might have been struck by the apoplexy. "*Sprechen zie Deutsch,* Wilbur?"

"What?"

He said it again. Then he went on. "That's German for 'Do you speak German?'"

"You get that out of a book?"

"Did."

"You speak German now, for God's sake?"

That sloppy puppy smile of his, then: "Just a little bit. There was a book in the crate. *Phrases for the Traveler in Europe.* Germany's in Europe."

"You goin' to Germany?"

"Probably not."

"Then how come you're learnin' German?"

"Learning is its own 'how come,' Wilbur. That's one thing came clear up here for me. You don't necessarily learn a thing because you can lever that learning to accomplish a thing. When you learn a thing, the learning is the accomplishment all by itself. Unless it's about knitting or baking pies."

I took a pull on the bourbon. I wasn't liking any of this. The Billy Piper I was talking to wasn't the Billy Piper I left behind the whole long time ago. I was losing my pardner, in a way. Didn't sit well with me. "Why would you ask somebody if they spoke German *in* German? If they didn't, they wouldn't understand what you're saying."

"Well, if they wouldn't know, then that's how you would know."

"Dammit, Billy, you're doing riddle talk again."

He laughed at that, drained his cup, went on talking, looking at all the books in the crate and making gestures in their direction, like you'd do if you wanted to make sure nobody felt left out of the conversation. The book was his friend and he was trying to introduce his new friend to me, was what it seemed like. Doncha see, Wilbur, I kept hearing him say, and he'd tell me about one of the books and the people who wrote them. Defoe and Whitman and Longfellow, who I'd at least heard of. Doncha see, Wilbur? Doncha see? Well, I didn't, not the way he wanted me to. What I saw was that he had himself a new friend and I thought that was my job. I told myself I'd keep working at it, that I wouldn't jump too quick, that maybe Billy was telling me a thing that was true and that I ought to know about, but remember what I said about the West not being a place that was easy with complications. That was still so, to my way of thinking, and the books that had Billy thinking like a still-wet Baptist come up from the crick looked to me like they was going to complicate things.

We drunk ourselves to snoring, and first light was a painful process for us both. We loaded up the high-sider, which didn't take long, being as a lot of what we carted up had gotten used away and a good deal of the rest could stay in the shack through summer. Billy was stubborn about the books needing to go on back to Salt Springs, except the knitting and baking ones. We put out feed for the thirty or so head Billy had rounded up for Starett. Wasn't a lot, wasn't a little, and the beeves wasn't the real reason Starett sent Billy on up to Jupiter View anyway. We tied Geezer and Whiskey to the ass end of the high-sider, and we was headed down the road by eleven, no need to turn a look back to see who got left behind. Billy and me'd done so much talking getting rid of the bourbon, there didn't seem to be much for us to say going back down. The air was warming, the woodpeckers were hammering hard, and it felt like quiet was a good thing for both of us to hear. Of course, right then I couldn't know that would be the last time I'd ever get a chance to feel like that about a new springtime, but that part I better save for later.

Billy reached over and pulled back on the reins when we came over the slope that gave us our first look at Salt Springs down in the belly of the gouged-out valley. The horses pulled in and Billy shook his head back and forth while he looked down there. "It's bigger," he said. "Least, I don't recall it spreading out so wide when we come up here last."

"Told you that, pal. It's all spread out more since the oil talk got real. More changes than brand-new twins. Starett's even talked to Heflin about being the law in town. Says we'll get big enough to need a lawman full time."

"Sheriff Heflin, for God's sake?"

"Don't think they're clear on what to call him. Marshal or Sheriff or Constable or who knows. But that's just one of the things they're talking. They say the railroad's likely to extend out even. That means depots and railway people and that means families, which means a school and then a teacher full-time, like Heflin, the law officer. They're talking new stores, and that means builders and that'll mean—"

Billy put a hand on my arm. "Tell me the last part again."

Damn, he was different. Had a bite that really clamped down. "They said there'll be stores needing to get built and they'll need carpenters and people like that. Builders."

Billy shook his head. "Not that part, Wilbur. Tell me the part about they're going to have a school and that means they're likely to be needing a teacher."

V

Heflin didn't want any part of being anything like a lawman or a constable or anything that they eventually decided to call the job. He told me that when him and me was unloading the book crate out of the high-sider. We'd sent Billy on to put Whiskey and Geezer into the corral. It was just too hard for Billy to deal with the book crate, what with the gimpy left leg of his. Heflin didn't like that Billy wanted the book crate in the bunkhouse instead of back into the Starett's. Seems Billy wanted to read some of the books over again, which seems like saying the first time was pretty much wasted time, but that was just him now; wasn't him before.

"I don't give a gopher's hump who breaks the law, unless the law they break busts into my pocket or bloodies my beak. Person starts pinning a badge on, he's just pinning on a target for a lot of those Hickoks out there and I don't want it, not a bit."

"You know how to handle a gun pretty good," I told Hef.

"'Pretty good' is plenty good for making coffee or pumpin' on a dove, but 'pretty good' when it comes to thumbing back a hammer and drawing down on another man is just an undertaker invite. No thank you."

"You tell Blackthorne?"

"Told Mr. Starret. He said he'd pass on the word."

"He say who they might look to get once Blackthorne finds out you decided to live out a long life?"

Heflin grinned, gap tooth and all. He nearly lost his hold on the book crate. We was almost to the place by Billy's bunk. "He said they might ask Willard Ganeel."

"Shit on a duck."

"Wilbur, I'm serious. That's what they're thinking about. Starett said Willard's always had the scattergun behind the counter. He hardly trusts anybody except his mother and she's been ten years dead."

We put the book crate down and straightened up slow, hands to our lower backs, both groaning like a pain choir. "Suppose Willard Ganeel turns them down, too. Who they going to ask then?"

"Willard won't turn 'em down. Shiny star. Sheriff Ganeel. Marshal Ganeel. He'll swell up and float off over the ridge when he gets that job. You watch. Month after he gets that job, he'll be wearin' a tie-down holster."

"Folks'll laugh."

"They'll laugh once maybe. Willard won't give them cause to laugh twice."

"Damn," I said. "This town's getting to be like a drunk running downhill, goin' more pell-mell with each step, till he falls splat on his face."

Hef offered up a soggy brown clump of chewing tobacco. Man with a gap tooth chewing tobacco isn't likely to rival a sunset. I'd rather chew on a dead cow's udder. Shook my head. He crammed a fistful into his craw, gummed a little bit. Said something. No way a human ear could make out what he said, so I just nodded. Hef chortled juice from the back of his throat and nodded, too, so it looked like the nod was presently in style. Heard the door open behind me and turned around to see Billy Piper standing there.

"I got me back wages coming for the winter, and once I see Mr. Starett, I'll stand for beers at Rooney's if anybody's interested."

Anybody was interested.

Hef and me waited in the little outside room when Billy went in to get his wages from Mr. Starett and tell him all about what he got done up on top of Jupiter View. We could have gone in and waited in the little sitting room off to one side, but the chairs and such Mrs. Starett had put in that room were all delicate with little curlicue legs, and neither one of us felt like our rumps were right for those fancy cushions. There was free beer at the end of the trail, so we could stand, we could wait. And we could also hear what Billy and Mr. Starett was saying to one another.

"Damnation, Billy," Starett was saying. "Thirty-two head. That's twice as many as I would have thought." You could hear from his tone he was smiling from ear to ear.

"I think you ought to count thirty-one, Mr. Starett. There was that one I told you about, sickly as can be."

"Billy, if it was sucking in air and blowing it out when you and Wilbur come down, I'm counting it in the mix. You earned your wages, son. Got it coming to you."

"Well, that's good, sir, on account of I figure it's going to cost a little more to live in Salt Springs upcoming." I could hear in Billy's voice that he was putting on his grown-up rig. He didn't do it very well, but I give him sand for trying, especially with Mr. Starett.

"Why do you think that?"

"Wilbur was telling me all the plans about new people coming in, new places going up, new homes and new stores and all. Seems to reason that with all the new people, that prices for just about everything might pop higher."

A negative growl from Starett. "You're wrong

there, boy. All the new people and stores and the railroad and the oil derrick gangs, that'll mean more competition, and that's what drives prices way down. Makes it better for everybody. Greases the wheels."

"That work for everything, the competition part?"

"Does. You bet it does."

"How's it going to work for the school part?"

"The what?"

"Heard they might be needing a school for all the railroader kids and clerk kids and all the kids, and I'm not sure how a new school slides into the competition box you're building."

There was a long time without talking, and I could easy see how Mr. Starett might be tilting his head to one side, looking at Billy like you'd look at a butterfly with horns. "How come you're so interested, Billy? You're a little old to be goin' to school, to my way of thinking at least."

"Mine, too."

"Well, then—"

"I was thinking to put in for being the teacher, sir."

Heflin coughed loud. I think he let some of his chew slide down. He looked at me, gap-toothed and chew-stained and hammered hard by what Billy just put out there.

Billy was telling Starett he didn't expect to just be handed the job, but that he's found out up on Jupiter View just what learning was all about, how it flamed up parts of his brain and how excited it come over him. He lost the grown-up stuffed-up sound and he was just Billy, telling Starett all about the books, all about being outside at dawn to catch the first gleaming so he could get back to reading what he'd put down when the night's cabin fire died. Then he told Starett about the Indian.

"Don't know how old he was, no way of telling, but he was old for a fact and I only knew he was coming past because the snow was new and each step he took had the scrunching whistling noise. He had rawhide britches and a blanket and there was icicles hanging down from his hair and eyebrows even. As soon as I saw him, I waved him to come on in, because he was walking, but he was walking frozen as it gets. His eyes and face were dead in the way he looked, and he just moved his head back and forth when I called out and pointed to the inside of the cabin. He just moved his head back and forth and turned his back, moving into the shadows, black as prairies pits. Don't know if he got himself turned out or if he wandered off on his own. What was sure was that he couldn't do what he used to do and wasn't willing to settle for a place in the circle he didn't earn. There was a bright moon that night he went by, but the clouds were everywhere so that was the way the moonlight was, too, soft over all there was, but more like cool noontime, with no shadows, and the farther off he moved, the more it was that the moonlight seemed to be shining right on through him, and I swore he got to be nothing but lines and dark parts the farther off he got, and that's when it settled in on me. Most time, I don't think we learn a thing quick, like you'd go and strike a match. Most times, it soaks into us with our hardly knowing a thing is happening, until it's happened and we get the point that we know something we didn't know before, that our thinking goes in a new place than it went before. That wasn't what happened with me while I was looking out into the night to the old Indian.

"Hit me like a bolt, it did, that him and me were exactly the same, that neither one of us could do what we'd always done before, and that I couldn't rightly claim to earning my place around the fire anymore, just like the Indian. And I knew I'd get put somewhere, maybe swamping out behind the bar at Rooncy's, or even worse'n that over at Honey's, and those kinds of things are just heart-cutters, Mr. Starett. Bleed a man from the inside out. It's being dead with lots of ladies' rouge on your cheeks. Not a way to be. Not a way.

"That's how I come to think about putting in for the teacher job, Mr. Starett. I know it sounds crazy to you, crazy to everybody you'll tell it to, and I don't bristle about that. But I do know how much I know, Mr. Starett, and I know how to learn more, more than I never knew was out there to know. And I'm easy with you talking to other teachers and having tests and finding out their experience and where they've done teaching, and each and every one will have done more teaching than me, because like we both know, I haven't teached anybody anything. But, there's the kicker, Mr. Starett, here's what I can throw in the pot that I bet the others can't, because they've been riding that rail for a longer time than me. You ride long enough, you'll get a callus on your backside. You teach long enough, you'll start to fall asleep in the saddle. Got to be. But not with me, Mr. Starett. Not with me. Those other teachers might be able to hand out bushels of facts I can't get to yet, but there's one thing I can teach that I bet they forgot all about.

"Mr. Starett, I can teach learnin'. Because I'm more tadpole than frog, I can teach how bright that light is and how it can make you warm before you ever knew you were cold. I can teach that, Mr. Starett. I can teach learning."

I saw a wild-animal circus once where they had a dog knew how to walk a stringy rope they had stretched between two poles. The look I had on my face then was the same look I was giving Heflin in the little room where we stood outside, listening. Neither one of us ever heard Billy talk that long a time at one go. Told you he was different.

There was an empty time before Mr. Starett spoke up. "Billy, I think you're trying to walk up a road that's frozen solid, but I'll pass on the word to Blackthorne and the others and I'll try

to see that you get treated fair." There was a
sound of crinkling paper. "Here's your wages.
You did good."

Billy came out of Starett's room a second later,
cramming the bills into his pocket. He looked
back and forth between me and Heflin. He knew
we'd been listening.

Billy smiled a little. His shoulders hitched.

"The man didn't say no," said Billy Piper.
"Let's get over to Rooney's."

We went to Rooney's, though I couldn't swear
up to it in court. I remember Hef and the Dutchman loading me across Geezer's butt and tying
me onto the horn for the ride back to Starett's. I
do remember walking in to Rooney's with Billy
and Hef, but it gets pretty smeared up after that,
which isn't my usual way, at least not on the past
ten, twelve years. There was a time I enjoyed getting squiffed more than just about anything,
squeaky springs singing with a purpose, but
when the years started adding on, I couldn't get
back to form as quick as I did younger. So I
reined that part of me in, until last night, and
why I went stupid last night, I didn't really know,
though there's a part telling me it's tied up with
Billy Piper, though that doesn't hold sense much
when you turn it this way and that and look at it
in the light. It's not like Billy Piper was my son or
brother or anything like that, where his changing his talk and thinking would cause me any
bother. We're just pardners a little. We just both

work at Mr. Starett's. He's not my brother, he's not my son.

I guess Hef and the Dutchman carted me in and put me on the bunk, but they didn't peel off my britches or shirt, for which I don't blame them, being as my skin nowadays looks like pie crust in the rain and I'm told that when I'm drinking stupid I give off a stench that you could nail to the wall. I woke up when my belly started bubbling, and I barely made it out the door before I started anointing the grass in just about every way you can imagine, though it's not an imagining I'd encourage you to do.

After a time, I teetered over to the trough and dunked my head under, swishing my mouth, spitting, dunking again. Any horse to drink out of this in the morning's sure to go at least blind, if he doesn't get mercy and just die. I come up, pulling in air as deep as I could, still not done with my shitting. And all this because of something I did to myself on purpose. I'll be eating turds next.

"Hey, Wilbur."

It was Billy's voice, soft as the night itself. Don't know why I didn't hear him close in. "Hey, Billy. You just gettin' back?"

His head moved up and down, once each way. "Me and Pearline had a lot of catching up to do."

"You get it all done?"

"Most, not all. Try again tomorrow night." He nodded off in the direction of the corral. "Geezer still was saddled when I rode in. I took it off. It's on the rail there with the blanket. Never saw you forget to do something like that before."

"I didn't forget. Heflin and the Dutchman must have. They rode me in and poured me to bed. They might have been a little squiffed, too. Lord knows I was."

He smiled a little. "Yeah. Looked like you were heading there when I left for Honey's. You were even starting to sing."

"Shit on a duck."

"You were, Wilbur. You were. Something about an Irish shepherd boy."

"Shit on a duck." And it come to me then, me standing on a chair, singing like a man yelling fire, Hef trying to bring me back down to the floor level. Something else needed to be talked on. This was getting too tight around my collar. "You tell Pearline about this notion you got about teaching school?" His head cocked off to one way, looking to me sideways. "Don't you look to me like that. You know damn well me and Hef could hear."

"I did."

"So, Pearline said . . ."

"Nothing."

"You told her you were looking to teach school and she didn't have anything to say to that?" I gave a snort in response.

"Not in words, she didn't," Billy said.

"What the hell's that mean?"

His mouth pursed up while he dug for words. What he found was this. "It means there's times and places where what gets said doesn't get said with a voice using words, and me and Pearline were in one of those times and one of those places."

"Oh."

"Bet your ass 'oh.'" He looked at me, shaking his head. "Wilbur, I got to say it. There's a smell coming off you a skunk wouldn't claim as his own. Jesus."

"Don't take the Lord's name in vain."

"Don't smell up the night and I won't." We both grunt-laughed at that and fell into step, moving back in the direction of the bunkhouse. Just the sound of our boots crunching and a few way-off hoot owls. "Ask you something, Wilbur?"

"You just did."

"And you haven't said a word about what I'm trying to do here. Like to hear your thinking on it."

"Actually, Billy, you probably don't."

"Hard card to play?"

"Is indeed."

"Play it anyway."

There was a belly avalanche building in me. Never again. I swore it. Never again. But there was Billy's question still floating there in the dark. "Billy, I only had a feeling like this once in my life when it came to you."

"When was that?"

"The second just before your ass settled down on Black Iodine."

"You damn well stink."

"It's my honest thinking on it."

"Not talking about your thinking, Wilbur. I'm talking about your stinking, which you do. Piss and puke and Lord knows what all. You need to get yourself down to One Legged Indian Crick and dip yourself good. Get buck naked and dip good."

I couldn't stop a shiver running through me. "Billy, that water's cold. My nuts'll be up around my ears."

"Then they'll be right next to your brain, and that won't be any big change for either one."

And that was when an important thing started to get clear for me, and this is what that thing was: When a person starts into that reading ringaround and putting new words and thoughts into their heads, those new things need to get tested out in the fresh air, and when they get tested out, they show up as smart-ass sassy back talk. Might be better, might be worse, but it sure as hell ain't the same.

My hair was still sopping from my time in One Legged Indian Crick when the Dutchman clawed my shirtfront and was dragging me on out to the front, saying that Hef wanted us to be riding fence on the South Fork, Hef's thinking having to do with the road running out there that the railroad people was coming in on. Hef said any break in the fence might offer too much shortcut temptation to the railroad folks and that wouldn't be right of us to do, tempting new neighbors like that.

Being with the Dutchman was a lot like being alone. With the exception of not being able to blow back gas without much worry about being too close. The Dutchman was a good worker, but he didn't have much to say, though he knew English good enough and he bellowed it out behind a closed crib door at Honey's.

We were on our third day out. Didn't see Billy for any of that time, of course, but Heflin told me later he put Billy to work getting the tack room cleaned out and ready to go, and that Billy did a fine job of it, still with his nose in a book every lunchtime and night until the lantern couldn't fight off the darkness anymore. Cookie was on the short side with Billy, mainly because Billy kept bringing him those cookbooks of Mrs. Starett's. Hef said he thought it was because the books served up an insult to what Cookie was stirring up for the boys each night, but I had me a different thought, which was that Cookie couldn't read a word in them books, or any other, and he didn't want anybody to know that fact.

The Dutchman and me were making good time on the fence, and planned on heading back the morning of the fourth day. Knowing we had that

coming, the night of the third day was a restful
time, rabbit on the fire, coffee hugging the coals.
Sun slipping down. Woodpecker hammering nails
into the gloom. Cowboy life has its points, pard.

"What's that there?" the Dutchman said. He
pointed off and I looked in the direction of the
pointing.

It was a wagon train of a sort, with maybe
fifteen wagons all told, heavy wagons, freight
wagons, each one of them with a big black
design on the side, the railroad name curlicued
into the design. The horses were leaning hard
into the traces, snorting and breathing deep.
They were pulling heavy loads they were, and
it wasn't often that heavy loads got teamstered
into Salt Springs, but maybe that's just the railroad way.

"What's in 'em, ya think?" the Dutchman said.

"The wagons, you mean?"

"Um." That was a Dutchman yes.

"Survey things. Map things. Road-planning
things. Just things."

"How come? Just for the oil?"

"Oil's money, Dutchman. Money's like manure.
It stinks up the air and the stink brings the flies.
We're looking at the flies." The line of wagons just
kept coming. The wheels rutting through, the
skinners bitching and swearing and hawing them
on. They could probably see our fire from where
they were, but I didn't see any of 'em take special
notice. They were pointed to Salt Springs, and it

looked to me like they might just keep right on going through the new night. The smell of that manure must be awful strong.

Some people are always downwind of that shit.

I had it right. They had got right on going through the night on their way to Salt Springs, and by the time two days later when me and the Dutchman rode back into town, there was already a little encampment, tents mostly, but with some having flooring shoved up off the ground and most having little pennants flying off from the tent peaks with the same railroad name and design we saw on the sides of the wagons. They'd laid in provisions and were getting themselves organized for a considerable amount of staying. There was a considerable number of the little survey telescopes on the three-stick stand-ups, and all the telescopes was polished and shiny as a gambler's glass eye. I asked the Dutchman what he thought, and he said "Um" again.

The envelope was propped up on the blanket wrapped on my bunk in the Starett bunkhouse. The lettering on the envelope was in thick black ink, printed stick-figure-like: *Wilbur Moss.* I looked around at the rest of them there, looking to see if I saw a smirk letting me know they was running me off to find a snipe, but nobody was doing anything to signal that. I opened the envelope and perched on the side of my bunk. I read.

DEAR MISTER MOSS:

I WOULD APPRECIATE YOU STOPPING BY THE
GENERAL STORE TO TALK OVER THE IDEA OF
YOU FULFILLING YOUR CIVIC DUTY TO SALT
SPRINGS.

KINDEST PERSONALS,
MARSHAL WILLARD GANEEL

I read it over a lot of times; finally just the last
part, which I stared at for a buncha ticks. Marshal
Willard Ganeel. Mother Superior Whore. General
Running Ass Scared. Marshal Willard Ganeel.
There's some words aren't supposed to be leaning
up against one another, and the three words
at the bottom of the letter I was holding were in
that same hole in the outhouse. Marshal Willard
Ganeel. Shit on a duck. I musta mumbled something or another, because when I looked up at the
rest of the boys, they were on board with what
I was thinking. Told me that Willard got himself
appointed marshal while me and the Dutchman
was riding fence.

"Appointed? Appointed by who?"

"The town council."

"The town council? Who the hell got on the
town council?"

"Starett and Blackthorne."

"Who appointed them to be on the town
council?"

"Starett and Blackthorne appointed themselves."

There'd never been a lot of questions inside me about whose town this was, and now it looked like there wasn't any room for any questions at all. And when I turned it over a few times, I started to see why there wasn't any new mayor for poor Salt Springs. Whoever was mayor would be looking back over his shoulder to the one who wasn't, and the one who wasn't the mayor would be edging around to climb into that chair. But when they split it straight down the center, they'd be looking out for each other and walking through each door back to back, making all their appointments, like Willard, and plumping up all the oil and railroad people along the way.

Once oil happened in town, I kept hearing folks telling each other that change was a good thing. I seen a lot of the change. Hadn't seen much of the good. Felt like things were happening more and more quick, but that there wasn't any clear road we were on, that moving was all that was needed, any direction, any way, any gain. Seemed like we were trying to pee in a windstorm. It'll all get out, but it might get sloppy.

In the General Store, there was a room at the back where ladies would go to try on whatever had taken their fancy. There was no sign, no anything on the door. If you went to the General Store, you knew what that little room got used for. But there was a sign on that door now.

It said: MARSHAL WILLARD GANEEL, with a white painted star over the letters.

Willard was wearing the star badge when I walked in to see him, and there was shiny wax on his mustache now, too. I never remembered him with a gun and holster when he was just clerking, but there was one on his hip now. Red leather on the holster. Gunmetal gray on the pistol. Handle looked to be bone. Willard called over his helper, and him and me went back to the room where the ladies used to try on their clothes. There was a sweet smell in the air, a lavender kind of echo, and I couldn't help thinking of a time when the room had a better use.

"Let's get to it, Wilbur. You interested or not?"

"In what? Interested in what?"

"I can't be everywhere at the same time. Being marshal is an important job. I'm going to need a deputy." He looked like a new bride putting out her first cherry pie.

And me not hungry. "You talking about me, Willard?"

"'Course."

"No."

"No? Who the hell are you to say no?"

"Who do I have to be?"

He drew himself up, like he'd sat down on a finger. "Don't you even want to know how much it pays?"

"If I'm ever expected to walk into Rooney's and pull out some fuzz cheek who's trying to prove he's got a pair by puttin' holes in my body where my body doesn't now have any holes, then it don't matter how much this job pays, because it couldn't ever pay enough for me to go anywhere and do anything like that."

"You got the wrong idea about this job and what we're looking for you to do. You wouldn't ever be asked to do anything like that. Besides, you wear a sidearm. You must know how to use it."

"Willard, about three days ago, I killed a rabbit with this gun."

"Well, there you are. You must be pretty good. Rabbits are quick."

"I hit him over the head with the butt of the pistol, Willard. For all I know, there's a mouse nest in the barrel of this fucking thing." I was slowing him up, and that was good. "You said about the job that goin' into Rooney's wasn't the kind of thing 'we're' looking for you to do. Who's the 'we' part of this deal?"

"Don't bone me, Wilbur. You know who it is. It's Fergus Blackthorne and Mr. Starett. Matter of fact, your name came up from Mr. Starett."

"Why? He tell you?"

"He did. Said you got a steady head, be easy to get on with. Knew the kind of town we had and how we didn't want people throwing rocks in our pond. Same thing he said about Billy Piper. Same reason we took Billy on to run the school."

Lord God Almighty, they gave Billy the job. Lord God Almighty. Willard hadn't stopped talking, but I was so spun around it took me a time to catch up.

". . . said the same thing about the both of you, that you'd go along to get along and we was at a time when getting along was an important thing, because we were at a place where that was an important thing. That's when he said the part about not throwing rocks into the pond. I didn't understand that at first."

"So, Billy gets the school-teaching job because he wouldn't be giving anybody any trouble."

Willard's head bobbed. His mustache shined like he dipped it in snot. "Same reason you got your job, Wilbur."

"I hadn't said I'd take the job, Marshal Ganeel." He liked it that I'd called him that.

"You turning it down?"

Stood there in what used to be the ladies' changing room without a right-angle thought in my skull. "I might need to talk to Billy about it. You got any idea where he might be?"

"Said he was going out to the railroad camp and see how many had families coming out with kids. After that, he was going out to the Pecker Draw. Starett said he's let Billy have the flatland there to build up a schoolhouse. Starett thought you might want to help Billy at doing that."

From cowboy to deputy to part-time carpenter. I wondered if I ever had a plan that didn't gallop off the cliff with me in the saddle. I shuffled off to the door, then turned back, peering hard at Willard Ganeel and his badge and his gun. I asked him how much the deputy job paid.

He told me.

It wasn't even close to bein' close.

I found Billy out at Pecker Draw. He was hammering stakes into the ground, wrapping strings around them, using the strings to lay out an outline of what he thought the schoolhouse ought to look like. Whatever it was going to look like was looking like it was going to be half a barn or better. There was string outlines for two outhouses behind, one for the girls, one for the boys. He was slick with sweat and smiling like a birthday child. He heard me coming up on Geezer, waved me on over. "Hey, Wilbur! You showed up right when I got all the work done."

"It's a gift I got." I reined in Geezer when we got close to the strings laid out. Stood up in the stirrups looking it over. He was standing there looking up at me, waiting. "Big," was all I said.

Billy pulled out a folded piece of paper and handed it up to me. "Got to be," he said. "Take a look."

I unfolded the piece of paper and what I read there was this:

Mary Mae Cawper, 9
David Disalle, 11
Elizabeth Forrester, 9
Cynthia Gorman, 13
Bobby Bo Jensen, 7
David Lundstrom, 14

Louise North, 10
Marcus Quint, 8
Mary Quint, 6
Addison Samuels, 15
Theodore Zachary, 10

"My first class," Billy said. "Or, at least, the first half or thereabouts." The look on my face must have had that slowest-hound-in-the-pack frame around it, so Billy went on. "Those are the kids of the railway people who've got wives following them on up here. Stands to reason the oil engineers will have about that many, give or take, and if that's so and I just double the railroad part, there's likely to be twenty-four or five in the class. At least, right around that number. That's a lot. Needs room. Not to mention when we add in Rooney's kid and Nicholas."

When you get to be carrying as many rings around the trunk as I carry, you know enough to start yelling about a cloudburst as soon as you see a thunderhead building up. You know some of them just pass on over, some of them get blown off in another direction altogether. But as soon as Billy mentioned Nicholas tied in with his school plans, I saw a big black thunderhead on the horizon, a collection of cauliflowered darkness all rolling over on themselves and seeming to be getting bigger with each passing tick.

"Bet you didn't even know he'd be around, did you?" Billy said.

"Who's that? Who didn't I know about?"

"Rooney's kid. Most people don't even know he's got one. Lives out past the junction with Rooney's older sister. She's been teaching the kid, but she's about done what she can do, barely reading very good herself. I got it that Rooney's glad to have him out from under."

Where Billy was looking, all he could see was sunshine and bright blue. "You going to build this up all by yourself?"

He shook his head. "Mr. Starett's going to split off some of his boys when it suits. And Mr. Blackthorne told Willard to have his deputy put a shoulder to the wheel, too."

"Well, I guess that'd be me."

A dove landed on Billy's lips and turned itself into a feather-soft smile. "You, Wilbur? You agreed to be deputy?"

"I plan on it, yeah."

"Damn-damn-damn. Why? What got in to you, Wilbur?"

I wondered how many times in my day I'd said something like that to some wrinkled-up cuss, and how many times that old cuss knew if he said the truth I'd spit on his boots, so he didn't tell me the truth, that all those wrinkles were like chapter headings that had knowledge I couldn't even barely dream of. So I did what an old cuss does when a wet-eared young buck starts telling you how good things are going to be and that the road around the corner is smooth all the way to the watering hole. I heard all that hope from

Billy and did what an old cuss does in times like that, which is that I looked him square in the eye and lied and lied and lied. Live long enough and you'll get to be real good at that.

"I'm just too old for this cowboy crap, Billy. I got a rump that's made out of solid bone boils. My butt and a saddle sounds like two rams locking horns in season. And 'tween the two of us, I got me a bladder that's shrunk up considerable. I pee now about as often as I scratch my nose. That don't lend with riding drag or even out mending fence."

He cocked his head to one side. "But I never knew anyone liked cowboy'n more'n you. Never."

"Never's one of those words don't apply to real life, Billy. 'Sides, I'm gettin' just weary of the life overall. I've done pretty much everything a man can do at bein' a cowboy. It's a little boring, to tell you the truth. The notion of being deputy, even to someone as lunkheaded as Willard Gancel, is kinda interesting. Like a challenge to me, like living a kind of life I never dreamed I'd get a chance to live."

I was tellin' the truth; I just didn't know it right then.

VI

Working on that schoolhouse with Billy was one of the most joyous times I ever had in my life. I puzzled on that for a time, trying to see why that was. It wasn't that the work was easy, because we were straining our milk pretty much every day, what with getting the lumber cut and the foundation laid out proper, getting the measurements right, all the carpentry things that come with this kind of operation, all of which me and Billy have both done before.

We'd be out of the Starett bunkhouse when it was still soft gray sky shine, and out to the construction before the sun mopped off the dew. Sometimes, we'd be shoulder to shoulder and we'd trade lies and stories and what was coming for Salt Springs with all the switchbacks going on in Salt Springs. Billy was all ready to buy, talking about the school and all it was going to mean, saying there'd even be a library in three years. I was just me, seeing grit in the cream and just waiting for it all to go sour. And if we wasn't shoulder to shoulder, him up high and me down low, it was good just to be quiet, surrounded by sawdust and songbirds, and I coulda gone on like that for quite some time. And Billy coulda, too, and I know that on account of all the times he'd be singing to himself. Couldn't carry a tune or remember the right words, so it was hard to know what song it was he was back-shooting.

Some days, Pearline and Nicholas came out, bringing a take-along from Rooney's, which was lunch and welcome. We'd sit around on the lumber piles and open up the take-along, with Pearline making everything out like we were a family on a picnic. She was primrose pretty and Nicholas was energy with a bright smile, and for me, who never had a family, they were some of the best times we had. I'd find myself watching Pearline and smiling, just enjoying the sound of her voice, the way it piped and danced, hearing her laugh and watching her clap her hands when Billy would make some little joke. Sometimes, I'd be thinking back on stories I told when we were on a drive, stories about wide-open ivory women thighs and how me and all the boys would laugh, and I regretted telling those tales when I was watching Pearline put out some of those odd family lunches we shared. She was sweet, Pearline was, and I was glad she and my pard knew how well they fit up.

After we were done with the food, Billy and Nicholas would take Rooney's take-along tins down to One Legged Indian Crick to give them a rinse, and that was the time when I'd get to talk to Pearline. Not that it was so much Pearline I was talking to, but just that it was a female and not matterin' to me what Pearline did at Honey's; it was just that it was a little bit of a time when I could drink in some of the softer side. It was striking me that I didn't have an oversupply of knowing how much I missed that all my life. Cowboy'n don't dwell much on that side. Sometimes, not many, but sometimes, she'd talk about Honey and the life, and I remember me asking her if her and the other girls weren't a lot afraid.

"What of?"

"Pearline, somebody snuck in and killed that one girl, Rosalie. If I was Honey, I'd be nailing windows shut and hiring night fighters."

"Whoever did it went off, Wilbur. It's done."

"Maybe. Maybe not."

She looked over at me like there'd been a loud noise. "How come you'd say a thing like that?"

"There's law in town now, Pearline."

"Willard Ganeel isn't any kind of proper law. Everybody knows that."

"Everybody except Willard. He thinks that badge come down from Heaven on high."

"But you're the deputy. Isn't that so, Willard?"

"It is."

"You're the one who tells him what to do?"

"Other way around. He tells me."

Pearline looked down in the direction of One Legged Indian Crick. We could hear Billy and Nicholas talking and laughing. The voices were getting closer. Pearline stayed looking at the woods below, but when she talked, she was talking to me. "If Rosalie's hand hadn't been shaking so much, we wouldn't be having this little talk, Wilbur. Just remember that and do whatever you can to put Marshal Willard Ganeel on the sidetrack." She straightened her shoulders back and waved off to Billy and Nicholas. She moved off to them, never looking back at me, but I knew full well she knew I was looking at her. Pearline and me never talked about Rosalie ever again. No need.

After a time, what we were doing actually started to look like what we hoped. There was a frame up and a shape, and it was enough to make any ten-year-old boy groan and spit, because what was there was no doubt going to end up being a schoolhouse.

I'd stand there and look at it at the end of every day and that's when it settled in on me, why the whole project was bringing me so much righteousness within. Cowboyin' doesn't build a thing; you move the beeves from here to there and it's hard, harder than other folks can ever know, but when you get them to where they're going, all of a sudden it's done and over with and you mount up and ride on back to the place you started out from so long ago. You're just a little sore and hungover and that's the change; that's the change. But at the end of those days working with Billy Piper, I was able to stand there and see something strong and real and know I'd had a part of putting it there and that it would be there for a long time after I wasn't. I wished I had a woman to tell that to, wished I had a kid to brag to.

It was an item could be reached out to, touched, sniffed. You could rub your whiskers on it, lean strong with your backside and know it wasn't ever going to give way. I recall walking by city buildings and seeing where some worker had carved his initials in the wood or stone, and it wasn't up until this very time that I understood why: Here I was; here's what I did. I'd ask Billy. He would understand, but I'd ask. It was his schoolhouse more'n it was mine.

Way in the distance I heard Nicholas start to play on his sweet potato for him and Pearline on their walk back to Honey's. Schoolhouse to whorehouse. I guess we must like being in a house.

While Billy and me were getting seriously puffed up about what we were getting done with his schoolhouse, it looked pretty heifered next to the bull work getting done in the town itself. The tent city for the railroad people had a lot more frame walls you could see, and there was serious talk about adding a wing to Rooney's and having that be a gentleman's hotel for the oil people.

Everyone called all these things improvements for the town, but there was one bird hadn't landed on a branch yet, and that was the talk of moving Honey's way out from Salt Springs itself. The thinking here was that if there was going to be wives and families and kids straying through our place, that Honey's and what went on there wouldn't be all proper. Which was so, in its way, as Honey's didn't have proper anywhere on its here-ya-go. It wasn't like we didn't already have kids in town. We did, more than just Rooney's kid, and from what I saw and heard, they just looked on Honey's as the place where the men went to see the ladies, and when they got a little older, they knew why the men was going there, and any town where there was bulls in one pasture and cows in another wasn't shattering many secrets about getting sweaty and happy at the same time. Nobody asked me. I never had kids. Maybe that's the reason. Too much work lying to them all the time.

One night a couple of weeks into the schoolhouse building, me and Heflin and the Dutchman rode on into town, heading for Rooney's and maybe Honey's after that. It was almost like I was coming into a town I never seen before. They'd been dragging the street with a sled loaded down with stones so they could smooth out some of the oldest ruts. The front of Rooney's had been whitewashed, and there was a new sign dangling out front with a curly R at the front of the word

Rooney's and letting everyone know that the owner's first name was "Sean," which I found out later is said out loud like there's an H after the first S, Irish apparently not being as simple a language as American is. The boardwalk that ran along the front of every business on Main Street had been hammered new and flattened out some. And then there was the outlining on the front of Honey's, where the new sign was going to go up, which was going to be new named "Miss Honey's Bath House for Gentlemen." Maybe that would keep Mrs. Starett and her hovering Ladies Aid sorts at arm's length.

The inside of Rooney's was the same, if you don't count that it was a lot cleaner now. It was still too smoky and noisy and had itself a smell, but if any of that had gotten made different, it wouldn't a been Rooney's anymore. I don't much care for the place when you list it all like that, but there's still some ease to be taken when you walk in the door and see it just like you left it; Rooney's was what you know filled with who you know. That's a pillow that'll fit your head and soften the edges.

The Dutchman hammered an elbow into my ribs and nodded toward the back of the room, and once I looked in that direction, I let off my pissedness at being elbowed by the Dutchman, because there was Omar standing at the very end of the bar, smiling at nothing, but definitely very pleased with being Omar, which isn't an easy thing to justify. He saw us looking at him and started down toward us, holding his beer up high, like a tightrope walker with a balance pole. Heflin waved Omar on over and made a hole for him in the line along the bar. The Dutchman nodded and grunted in Omar's direction, so we wouldn't be hearing much more from him for the rest of the night.

"What the hell brings you in here, Omar?" Heflin said. "This boot don't fit you."

Omar's smile broadened out. "Saw him walk on in here. Had to come see how he was doing. Looked good. Had to find out for sure if he was good."

"Who're we talking about?"

Omar's head bobbed off to one side. Looking over there, I saw back into the little dining room Rooney kept for his specials. Shit on a duck, there was Billy sitting at one of the white table-cloths with Pearline, and a waiter was pouring pink wine for them both. Had to be the first wine for Billy. Pearline mighta gotten treated over to Honey's by some such lout. She was wearing a shiny satin, soft-blue-like, and there wasn't a soul in the place except them, at least as far as they were concerned.

"How the hell's Billy afford being back there?" Heflin said.

Omar replied: "Doesn't have to afford it; he's there on Rooney's treat."

"Rooney's treating him? When the hell'd

Rooney start treating crippled cowboys and their whores?"

The answer was mine and it made me happy and sad all at the same time. I knew why I was happy, but the sad kept itself in the shadows. "You got it wrong, Hef. Rooney ain't treating a crippled-up cowboy and a whore. He's treating the man who's going to be teacher of his son. He's treating the new schoolteacher and the schoolteacher's lady and don't you ever forget it." Heflin humphed and took a gulp of barley death, and I just kept watching Billy and Pearline. There wasn't a man in the front saloon who didn't know how Pearline padded her purse, and there was likely more than one man in the room who had laid some change on top of her dresser. She knew that and Billy knew that and still they kept firm in their traces, heading up their particular hill, pulling that load as best they could.

"Doin' fine, too, as well as I can tell." It was Omar talking all about Billy's leg. He said the bone wasn't set perfect, if you meant that "perfect" had to have "straight" in there, too. But it had set strong, said Omar, and while it might ache up on him sometimes, it ought to hold up for what he's got to do, and that's all anyone could expect, seemed to him.

Struck me that Black Iodine mighta freed Billy up in ways none of us could appreciate clear, but that thought went out of my head when Billy and Pearline got up from their table and moved off toward the front door. There was a back door to Rooney's, and they coulda headed there, but that didn't seem to be in their thinking. I caught their look and tipped the hat, waggled a few fingers. Billy nodded and Pearline smiled, fingers waggling back to me. It meant something to them that I waved. Meant something to me that they waved back.

Changed my plans for the evening, though. Couldn't have a friendly wave like that and then head on over to Honey's later and eat from the other side of the bowl. You don't do that. I don't know why, but I know you just don't.

I walked Omar outside after I stood him for a drink more and he started to show a serious list to port. He was pleased and he was proud and he was as squiffled as a man ought to be who holds the medical ability of the town in his hands. I knew Blackthorne and Starett were talking about the railroad and oil meaning that a diploma doctor would be pulling in most any day now, and I didn't know what that might do to Omar. No need to tell him now, nothing to be gained, so I pointed him off toward his place and he walked off, pigeon-toed and knock-kneed, but making more progress than not.

I peered off to the other side of the street when I heard twin boot strikes on the boardwalk there. Willard Ganeel was out making what I figured he'd call his night rounds. Fergus Blackthorne was by his side, hand on Willard's shoulder.

Willard had his left hand wrapped around the butt of his pistol. Even when Fergus would say something, Willard would just nod, never looking over, head swinging back and forth like a boat pilot on the Platte. They stopped when they got to the corner and talked a bit, Fergus mostly, and while I couldn't make out any words, the tones were easy and friendly, and Fergus's hand stayed on Willard's shoulder the whole while. There was a handshake, and Willard moved off down the right-angle street, leaving Fergus on Main Street. He was just starting to turn away when he heard the sound of Nicholas playing the ocarina. The moonlight was almost straight down, but there were still black shadows under the overhang and that's where Fergus scurried back to, standing there in the dark looking over at the second floor of Honey's.

Billy and Pearline were out on the deck, her sitting in the rocker. He was standing behind her, rubbing her shoulders. Pearline was wearing a veily robe and her hair was down. Nicholas was sitting on the railing that circled the deck. The song he was playing was the song you hear from a nightbird on the river. I looked back over at Fergus.

He wasn't moving, just looking up to the deck. Then he unbuttoned his frock coat and his right hand was at his front. It took a few ticks, but pretty soon I realized he was rubbing his hand up and down his front in that way every man knows, whether they want to own up to it or not.

Billy wasn't there when I got back to the bunkhouse, and he wasn't there when I woke up in the morning either. He mighta stayed the night with Pearline, but that didn't hold, bein' as while Rooney might stand you a meal if he was of a mind, Honey didn't run her enterprise in a way that I heard Mr. Starett call more suited to a lazy fair. So Billy came back after me and got up and left before me. Wasn't the first time. Been almost every morning lately.

He wasn't at the schoolhouse when I got there either, which was lately somewhere in between never happen and regular doing. He never said where he was spending the early part of the day and I never asked, but being as he made sure to stay later than me on those days when I got there and was working before him, I didn't have any call to push on him about it. This particular morning, though, it wasn't like that.

He showed up with a cloud on his face, and it stayed there most of the day. Wasn't any singing or stupid talk. There was just that cloud all around him and everything he did. I was thinking it might be that him or Pearline got wind of Fergus Blackthorne standing there in the overhang. I got pretty much certain of that when Billy and me were eating lunch.

"Talked with Blackthorne this morning," he said.

"Where'd you see him?"

Billy chewed on a stick. Spit out a chunk of bark. "I went over to his stables."

He said it like a coin flip, like I ought to know why he was there. He was wrong. "What was you doin' over there?"

"Givin' apples to Black Iodine." He saw my look. Smiled. Shoulders hitched up. "I been over doin' that the past couple weeks every morning."

"How come?"

"Make a friend."

"That friend crippled you up some, Billy."

"More'n some, I'd say."

"So, how come?"

Billy shook his head like there was a gnat buzzing around. It wasn't the question he didn't like. It was that the answer he had didn't have any hard corners to it. "I can't get a rope on it, Wilbur. It's just something I want to do. Or try to do."

"And Blackthorne saw you doing it and he'd rather grind the horse up for pig slop."

"No. We didn't talk about Black Iodine. We didn't talk about anything like that."

"What'd you talk about?"

"Nicholas not being allowed in the school."

And that was where the cloud got born and why it was so stubborn in getting blown away. Billy had given his list of students to Mr. Starett, and Mr. Starett had passed it on to Blackthorne, sharing information was all, and Blackthorne got creased every way you could get about it.

Told Starett the town was on a precipice, ready to leap across and step up to a whole new place, bring in new people, build out new businesses and shops and stores. Oil and railroads and mercantile, was how he said it, and according to Billy, Blackthorne said it to him, too, over and over, oil and railroads and mercantile. Like a Catholic stroking Latin the way they do, diving down into the sound and letting it cover their ears. Oil and railroads and mercantile. Nigra boy in a school full of white tadpoles would splash the pond and spoil the surface, he said. No, no, and no. I spoke the way you walk across a new frozen river. "Billy, what Blackthorne's saying might be the easiest way."

"The easiest way?"

"Might be, yeah."

"And that's good, keeping Nicholas out of school."

"Didn't say 'good.' Said 'easy.' And that's pretty close to what Starett and Blackthorne are looking for you to do."

His head swung around to me slow. Held on me for a long time. I felt me a need to get up, so I did.

"Better get a move on," I said. "We're burning off too much time. We can still get a start on those front steps, don't you think?"

"Sit your ass down, Wilbur."

"Billy, we got work to do."

He shook his head, held me like a pin holds a

dead butterfly. "You got talking to do, Wilbur. Maybe a little, maybe a lot. But you've got some talking to do, and there's nothing out here that's more important than any of that."

So I sat me down and started, telling Billy what Mr. Starett said, told him about not being high on the test list, but Blackthorne putting a pointer on him because he was a Salt Springs boy and he'd do what was right for the town, do what was right as far as Starett and Blackthorne decided right to be. Told him and told him and hurt him and hurt him with each word, each breath, hurt him in deep ways I don't think I ever hurt a man before. He stood up in the middle of it, fists balled up tight, jaw working, lips all stone. He stalked off as best he could, moving off in the direction of where he ground-tethered Whiskey.

"Go do it, Billy! Go find Blackthorne or Starett or both of 'em and give 'em each a snot-knocker for me! And tomorrow you'll be a gamed-up cowhand who can't ride and a schoolteacher who almost had himself a school and kids who needed teaching! Hell, you'll feel real good then!"

Billy'd just started the half jump he had to do to mount up since his left leg was too stiff to lift his foot the proper way into the stirrup. He was half belly over the saddle, looking back over his shoulder at me, feet dangling. Looked fairly humorous actually, but it wasn't the right time to point that out to him. He slid down off the saddle, stood there with his head resting against

Whiskey's flank. He turned around, looking at me in a way I didn't like at all. He walked back toward me, bobbing up and down a little with that wobbly walk of his. When he stopped, he was just a little closer than him and me usually stand with each other.

"Maybe I ought to start the snot-knockin' with you right here and now, Wilbur."

"Why would you want to do a thing like that?"

"Because we tell each other the truth, you and me, and you knew what they was saying about me and how I'd slip along."

"Billy, what they're looking for you to do is the same thing they're looking for me to do. I'm an old windbreak who they figure will do what they tell him not to do. You're a so-called teacher without a teaching paper in your back pocket. Way they see it, we're both stove in and not worth worrying about. We got nothin' to fight with, Billy, because we got no place to go."

He looked off from me. The fire got dampened. He took in a long breath. "Goddammit to hell and gone, Wilbur. Nicholas ought to be able to go to school. Everybody ought to be able to go to school!" He looked me direct again.

"Billy, don't start in on one of your learnin' sermons again. I—"

"Hell, Wilbur. You ought to go to school!"

"I can read menus and road signs. I don't need anymore."

"You don't know what you need, Wilbur. That

proves why you need to go to school." His smile a sad one, older than usual for Billy. He turned away and walked back to Whiskey, head down, the left leg coming along like a lost calf. He pulled himself up across the saddle, swung his right leg over.

"You want some help with the other foot?"

"No. I can do it." He got the toe of his left boot into the stirrup, tried to push it in farther.

I started over to help.

"Touch that foot and it'll be the last goddamned thing you touch." He worked the foot, standing up partway, then sliding it on into the stirrup in a way that worked. He whistled when it got done. Looked down at me. "So, we're doing what we're doing because they don't think we can do anything that's worth salt. We're doing what we're doing because we'll never put a stone in their boot no matter what."

"The way I see it, yeah."

"The way you see it makes some sense, Wilbur. Wish I didn't agree about that, but we're pretty much capons in all this deal, ain't we? We could just saw off our balls and put 'em in a safe somewhere." His heels touched on Whiskey's flank and the horse started forward.

"Where you goin'?"

He didn't look back when he talked. "When I got things to think about, I used to take a walk. That's not so easy anymore, so now I let Whiskey do the walking while I do the thinking part." The pony went on a bit; then Billy reined in and turned around in the saddle, looking back, "Tell you one thing, though."

"Waiting."

"One of the reasons to put our balls in a safe is to make sure we know where they are when the right time comes to pull 'em out and put 'em to proper use. So, don't you forget the combination to that, old man, 'cause they're coming out at the right time, I'll guarantee you that. They're coming out at the right time."

I stood there watching him and Whiskey move off into the woods, his game leg sticking out stiff. Made him look like an upside-down Y. When he was out of sight, I thought about heading back into town, but I was too dark to do that, so I looked around for something that needed doing on the schoolhouse, something that would let me feel it wasn't all so empty a day I was goin' through. We had trouble getting the steps level just right, so I went over and hung out a new plumb line, trying to get it right. Then I started to hear Billy yelling. I was over by Geezer, just starting to pull myself up into the saddle, when I realized the yells weren't about any kind of trouble or Billy needing help.

The yells were just him out there in the woods somewhere, bellowing and howling. No words, no anything but anger and head-butting bile and piss vinegar. Pounding the dirt probably, kicking at pine cones and rocks. There comes times when you just got to let the Lord know that you're not sure how much more you can take and He needs to start taking those fancies into account. It was hard to tell how far off Billy was. Things echo hard in the trees and stay in the air a long time. Wouldn't be a surprise to me to know that some of Billy Piper's yelling and bellowing was still bouncing off the trees on some mountainside to this very day.

He was doing his kind of work out there in the woods. It was time for me to get back to my job on the steps.

The next morning was like the morning before it, with Billy gone by the time I lifted my head off the pillow. Couple of seconds before it come to me that the mornings weren't really twinned up, because Billy had told me where he went once it got light.

And when I got there, there he was, one rung up on the stable's corral fence, with Black Iodine circling round, edging in a little closer each time. Though there wasn't no line, Black Iodine was definitely hooked. I stayed still, watching while it closed in on Billy's hand, stretched out to him, shining red apple held steady. Billy was making little soft clicking noises, like you might do for a squirrel or a pigeon. Lord knows why we think they must like clicking sounds. But maybe it's so, because in a while, Black Iodine's head was right opposite Billy, only a foot or so above that shiny red apple. Billy's hand was steady as a boulder at the bottom of a pond. He left off the clicking sounds. "Hey," he'd whisper. "Hey . . . hey . . . breakfast time's here . . . come and get it . . ."

Damned horse did just that. Bobbed its head down, grabbed the apple, and backed away, never taking its eyes off Billy. Barely a chomp or two, and then a throat wiggle and gurgle spit noise, and Billy was reaching into the belly of his shirt, coming out with a second apple.

First one musta been good. Black Iodine took a step toward him, stopped, then took a second one. Billy's hand was out like before and he was smiling easy and strong. The big horse took one more step, and Billy's left hand went around to his back pocket. He pulled out a little piece of cloth. Kept it all wadded up. Iodine's head had moved back into the feed chute again, and it was looking down at that apple. When it bobbed down to get its treat, Billy did two things in a blur. When the apple was out of his right hand, he gave the horse a strong pat on its neck while his left hand reached around and folded out that rectangle of cloth on the big stallion's back, right at the base of the neck. Iodine never quivered. There was an apple to get down the gullet. No time for a fainty feather on its back. Iodine moved away, jaws working, gurgling coming to the surface. Billy looked over and saw me, smiled, waved me on over. I came up to his side and we looked into the corral. Iodine might have been a spawn of death itself, but there was no denying the damned horse was the hugest piece of ebony that ever got turned into snorting sweaty horseflesh. The low morning sun danced off each little valley and muscle. If you'd thrown a buncha snakes into a black satin bag, them turning all around each other under that satin woulda looked exactly like the beast's muscles wrestling under his skin. Beautiful and dangerous, though maybe that's pretty much the same thing, when you get to the dark part of things.

"What the hell's that on his back?" It was Fergus Blackthorne who called out, coming out of the stable. He had a steaming crockery cup of coffee in his hand. "What the devil is that anyway?"

Billy nodded, pointed to himself. "That's mine, Mr. Blackthorne. That's my handkerchief."

"What's it doing on his back?"

"I'm just trying to get him used to the feel of a little something there. Just trying to show it won't hurt him."

"Jesus, Billy. Jesus . . . George on that one." He blew on the coffee, took a noisy slurp. "Never knew a cowboy who carried a hanky before."

Billy cleared his throat. It was a soft noise, the kind you do in church. "I'm not a cowboy anymore, Mr. Blackthorne. I'm a schoolteacher, remember?"

Blackthorne looked sideways at Billy. "Oh, that's right. You're a schoolteacher now. I forgot about that. I'll try to remember next time."

He bounced his look in my direction. "Wilbur, I don't see you wearin' a badge. Shouldn't a town's deputy be wearing a badge?"

"I got it back in my kit."

He took in a deep breath, hummed a little, letting it out. "We'll probably get into that tomorrow night, Wilbur, but I think you need to have that badge on all the time."

Billy looked a question over at me, and I looked back I-don't-know-either to him. "What's tomorrow night, Mr. Blackthorne?"

"We're going to have a meeting of all the town employees. You two are town employees now, you know. You and Willard Ganeel and Sarah Allgood. We're going to make her town secretary. Her handwriting's the best. Looks like it came right out of a printer's shop." He went to take a sip of coffee, but there wasn't any left. He looked at the bottom of the cup like there'd been a plot against him. "Anyway, Starett and me decided we'd have a town employee meeting to set policies and so forth. Things like wearing badges, things like that."

I'm not much for meetings, and I guess that showed on my face. I admire anyone who's got strong ideas and ways to tell you about those ideas, but it's always seemed to me the more people you get in a room talking about a problem, the more smooth and polite and watered down it all turns out to be. A hundred people can sing a song, but only one can sit down and write it.

"Eight o'clock in the General Store," Blackthorne said. "See you both there." He nodded an adios and moved off in the direction of his place.

All I could think of was him standing under the overhang in the darkness there, looking up at Billy and Pearline and Nicholas. I wished I hadn'ta seen it, because it wouldn't go away and it was in my head in a festering kind of way.

"Look," Billy said. He was pointing off to Black Iodine in the corral. "The handkerchief's still there."

"So?"

"If the handkerchief stays, then maybe a saddle blanket will stay. If the blanket can stay, then maybe there's a bit of hope for a saddle. Any saddle needs a rider. Might be a chance."

"Billy, your brains gettin' more crooked than your bad leg. You ought to want to kill that damned horse, not break it."

He stared out at Iodine for a long time. "Wilbur, you're part right. I do want to kill that horse. And that want is the very thing I'm trying to tame."

That didn't make a whole lot of sense to me, and I was getting too hungry for breakfast to arm wrestle with it. "Cookie was throwing slop together when I left. You want to go eat?"

He came down off the rail, shaking his head. "I'm going on over to Forrester's Smithy. Want to see if he's got a bell we can put up at the schoolhouse."

"Never saw a bell at Forrester's. Saw a come-to-dinner-triangle clanger there. That sets off a racket that's hard to ignore."

The head shake got shorter and more set. "No. A schoolhouse needs a bell. Church gets a bell for the same reason. It's an important place with an important reason."

"They got bells at funerals, too, sometimes."

Billy laughed, his smile like a crescent moon. "You making plans to go to a funeral, Wilbur?"

I said no, but of course I couldn't see what was coming.

Mrs. Ganeel put out a spread for us at the town employee meeting, and Willard had cleared off a place on the counter for all the plates and platters. What was there was side meat and johnny-cake and hominy, steaming away, filling the room with more warm closeness than might be hoped for. Willard kept saying that his wife could cook anything, and after the first bite of side meat and johnnycake, I thought that would-cook was a better fit than could-cook. The only thing that would eat that pig would be another pig. Sara All-good finished a first plate and most of a second. Sara was a husky woman.

Mr. Starett and Mr. Blackthorne came in a few minutes late, that being because they stopped to have dinner at Rooney's. I have noted in my time that rich men don't stand in line to be first for side meat and johnnycake. Coffee got poured and dishes stacked and everybody found a place to light. Starett and Blackthorne were at the front. Starett was the official talker.

"Folks, we're at a door here, and on the other side of the door is a room this town's never been in. It's a bigger room than we've ever been in before, and there's people in there we don't know, powerful people who can chew up the town of Salt Springs and spit it out again. That's why we've got to get us organized, get us thinking the same way and behaving the same way. We've got to make sure these other people take Salt Springs seriously and listen to what we have to say."

Sara Allgood made a little pigeon-coo noise. "Do you really think things are going to be all that different? Really?"

"Sara, it's going to be more different than you can imagine." Starett pulled off his half-glasses and used them to point to us all. Might as well have had a sign around his neck: something important coming up. "Let me give you an example, something Fergus and I just heard about a few minutes ago. You know about the supply barn the railroad's got at Twilly's Pass. All sorts of equipment there, stored up for the construction going on. Two puffer-belly switch engines there. I believe we're all here in accord with the notion that we have a good crop of young people. Oh, there's mischief, there's back talk, there's the occasional outhouse gets picked up and moved. But they're generally a good lot, well mannered, respectful, clean, mannered through and through. Anybody here doesn't think that's accurate?"

Nobody but Blackthorne knew what he was talking about, so we nodded.

"Well, let me tell you how this incoming boom has already affected our young people. Last night, somebody busted the lock on that supply shed and climbed up on top of one of those puffer-bellies and took off with the locomotive bell itself!" His fist smacked down on the counter. "Unscrewed it from the fitting and took off like a thief in the night!"

"Actually," said Blackthorne, "it *was* a thief in the night."

I peeked over at Billy. He was looking straight on at Starett. A pound of lime with white paint poured over would have showed more clue.

"But do we really know it was some of our young people?" said Sara.

"Miz Allgood, who on earth else could it be?" It was Billy doing the talking. "I did my share of mischief when I was green and growing. Some do; some don't. But it's the way of some youngsters. That's why I look forward to getting our school up and running. I understand what devilment can exist in a youngster. I understand it firsthand."

"And you think you could have an effect on this kind of thing?"

"Ma'am, I think I could turn it back like Moses did with the Red Sea."

Starett cut in. "Point is, our young people are being twisted around. The world's getting powerful more complicated and hard to understand. That's why we're all here."

"I'm here because I was told to be here." I was saying an honest thing. Honest and smart aren't always the same thing, seemed like.

Blackthorne looked at me hard. His eyes had the kinda glow you can see in a cougar's eyes in a dark cave. "And I see you're still not wearing your badge either."

"It's in my kit, Mr. Blackthorne. Keep forgetting the damned thing. Pardon the language, Sara."

"Well, Wilbur," Starett said, "you got to start wearing the badge full time. That's part of your job, showing people that we are putting together a town where the law stands firm and tall, a place where people can feel restful about raising a family. You don't wear the badge, you don't get paid. Let's put it that way."

"It's a strong way to put it, Mr. Starett. I can see a benefit to me wearing the badge more. I'll look to it."

"And Billy, we're clear about you and the colored boy, yes?"

Billy Piper nodded instantly. "He won't be going to the weekday school, Mr. Starett. Rest easy on that."

Blackthorne's head lopped over to one side looking to Billy. "Whoa in on that a bit. What's this 'weekday school' you're talking about?"

"Saturday. Saturday school. Nicholas and three or four of the girls from Honey's. And there's the Creole waitress at Rooney's is thinking about it as well." He didn't have any expression at all on his face. Looked like a frog who just ate a fly.

Blackthorne wasn't going to be that fly. "We're not paying you to teach on Saturdays, Billy."

"Oh, I know that. But the girls all agreed to do a little cleanup after we were done with class. And I can always find some little thing for Nicholas to do. It's all sort of a barter deal."

"And what exactly would you be teaching these people, if you don't mind my asking?"

"Reading, almost all the way. Nicholas don't have that at all, and all the girls are real ragged about what they can understand. Once they get reading down, everything else will pretty much fall into place."

Starett reached out and put a hand on Blackthorne's arm. It stopped Blackthorne from saying what he was going to say, which, judging from the size of the breath he took in, was going to be loud.

"Sara," said Starett, "I think you can go on home now. You surely understand what we're looking for in a town secretary and you're more than capable of doing the job. We need a little time to deal with matters that would just bore you. Man-talk issues."

She burbled up, pulling her shawl, taking up her big patterned bag. Man-talk issues wouldn'ta bored her in the least, but Sara knew the rules. "Heaven's sake, thank you. This is way past bedtime for me." She moved over to Warren on her way to the door. "You tell that wife of yours she's the queen of side meat as far as I'm concerned, and if she wants to share a recipe or two, just stop on by."

"I'll tell her."

"Don't see why you're not big as a house, married to a woman who cooks like that!"

"Worrying about keeping her helps me stay thin, Sara."

Sara laughed, a sound like a pipe organ with a leak in the bellows. She wished us all a good night, thanked everybody for their time and thoughtfulness, waited a little for a few more thank-you's, then squeezed out through the door.

While she was doing her farewell performance, I was looking at Billy and Willard Ganeel, and it was pretty clear that the three of us didn't have the map to what the other two had in mind when it came to the man-talk portion of the meeting.

"Fergus and I have talked," Starett started in, "and we've come to a mind about what we think ought to be the first regulation applying to employees of the township—"

"City," Blackthorne said.

"We haven't done those papers, Fergus, and we have to file papers with the capital before we can call out that we're a city."

The grunt Fergus gave out was not a congenial sound.

"Anyway, Fergus and I have come to an agreement about what we think ought to be a prime regulation for employees of Salt Springs." He stopped, looked to each one of us, not about to go on until someone asked the question that put an important frame about the picture he was trying to hang.

Willard was on it. "What would that regulation be, sir?"

"That no male employee of the township frequent the premises of Honey's. Might not look right to some of the new people settling in. Flies the wrong flag."

Willard was there again. "Won't change my ways at all, sir. I'm a married man."

"Not only a married man, but married to a fine cook, too, according to Sara." Starett smiled, trying to spread the mood. It was spreading, but like paint on a gritty board. The smile fell in my direction. "How about you, Wilbur? Aren't you getting a little too gray-groined for all that nonsense?"

I looked at him, then reached down into my vest pocket and pulled out the good watch I won five years back in Riverton. I clicked the case open and looked down at its face.

"What are you doing?" Blackthorne said.

"Trying to figure out how just what I do or don't do with the girls in Honey's got to be anybody's business but mine."

Blackthorne was all rattler. Starett still was wearing his smile. "Right is right, Wilbur, and you're the right one about this and I trust you'll accept my apology."

Blackthorne took it up that next second. "Just like we think you'll accept the fact that we've got the right to make regulations that apply to those people we're keeping on government payroll." He wasn't looking for an answer, didn't wait for one. Billy got the rattler look next. "How about you, Mr. Schoolteacher? Anything about this get in the way for you?"

"Guess it depends on how much you lean on the English language, Mr. Blackthorne."

"That a sentence with a meaning. Suppose you explain that to me."

"You and Mr. Starett talked about employees who frequent Honey's. What's the 'frequent' mean? That we can go there a little, but a little more than that might be too much?"

Blackthorne's lips got lemony. He looked at Starett, who looked at the floor. "What we mean, Mr. Piper, is that male employees of the township of Salt Springs shouldn't set foot on the other side of the door that leads into Honey's. One time is too many. Two times is two times too many."

"I'm a single man, Mr. Blackthorne. A young single man."

"Maybe you ought to start going to church."

"I do go to church, Mr. Blackthorne. Name of the church is Honey's."

I was just praying Billy wasn't going to tell what it was he worshiped in that church of his. Well, not praying, no.

Starett's voice was soft, trying to wrap the room in velvet. "Billy, it's no secret here that you've got a special hitch-up with one of the girls at Honey's. You ought to know that's not the reason for this regulation. We're just wanting to keep everything family-friendly. We're not just picking on you."

"One's married up. One's grayed out. And I'm the one left and you're not picking on me or anything like that."

"Exactly."

Blackthorne tried to chuckle. Didn't sound human. "Besides, Billy, it sounds to me like this Saturday school of yours might make your life a little sweeter when it comes to matters of the girls at Honey's."

"I came up with the Saturday school way before we had this meeting, Mr. Blackthorne."

"Well, that's not to say there won't be a little sneaking off into the woods when the shadows get long at the end of the day, is it?"

I glared at Billy with the tightest look I had, roped him in, and pulled the knot tight. It slowed him some. I said, "Seems to me you're telling us what you've already decided on and you're not asking for a vote, but just whether or not we'll get in line like you want."

"Well, if you want a vote, you got my vote," said new Sheriff-Marshal Willard Ganeel.

That was news like saying a rooster's got nuts. Blackthorne snuck an eye at Starett and Starett met it straight on. A nod from one gave the gavel to the other. Starett took in a deep breath, sighed, and talked. "Probably so, Wilbur. You need a little time to think this over, do you?"

"It's getting late, Mr. Starett. I'm an old wind-break. I go down a little slower than the sun, a little later, but when I feel like I'm getting dim toward the end of the day, it seems like waiting till a better sun checks in just has some sense about it."

We got done quick then. They said we could let them know tomorrow. There was thank-yous and more smiling lies about the quality of the side meat and johnnycake and hominy brought forth by Mrs. Willard Ganeel. I don't think she coulda had a job at Honey's under no circumstances.

Billy and me went out front, and he asked me to give him a boost up onto Whiskey, which told me how the news about Honey's had hit him. He swung his leg over and mumbled some kinda thanks, but he was slumped there when he said it, shoulders low, looking at the ground. When I started over to Geezer, I saw Willard Ganeel waiting there on the boardwalk. He waved me on over. "I'll catch up," I said to Billy.

"I'll wait for you," he said back.

I went over to Willard and he leaned in close, keeping his voice to a whisper. "Deputy, we need to start getting organized on this law enforcement matter."

"I'll wear the badge, Willard. Unclench."

"That's not my topic," he said.

"What is?"

"There was a murder committed in Salt Springs no more than two months ago and we have to get to finding out who done it."

"You're talking about the Coughing Girl."

"Certainly am."

"You're a damn brave man, Willard Ganeel."

Willard's brow got wrinkled. "How's that? How am I brave?"

"Well, whoever killed that poor girl just crawled in through that window and blew her brains out, Lord knows why. And when a fiend like that hears there's a professional lawman like yourself determined to track down a perpetrator, it stands to reason he'll think about doing the same kind of thing to that lawman or to those the lawman holds near and dear. A man's got to have bull balls to run that kind of risk, and there's no doubt in my mind but that Willard Ganeel is that kind of man."

There was a little twitch where his lips joined

up. Didn't move for the longest time. There was a little moan from somewhere in the back of his throat. Sounded like a bubbling teapot getting moved off the stove. "Just make sure you wear the badge from here on out, Wilbur." He turned and moved off down the walk.

I pulled my butt up on Whiskey and me and Billy started out back to the Starett place. I looked over at Billy. He was more himself now. Maybe he heard me and Willard. Maybe that helped. "We can work on hanging that front door tomorrow," I said.

His head rocked back and forth, lower lip all shoved out. "Nope. Not you, at least."

"How come?"

"I'll get the door hung. Got another job for you."

"And what's that?"

"I need you to build a tall strong tower where we can put up the school bell."

"Oh. You found a bell?"

"I did. I tracked one down."

It struck me as a little off gait for Billy to be telling me he wanted me to build a tower for this bell of his, but the next morning when I saw the bell, I started to understand why he wanted the bell to be in a high-up place. The lettering around the bottom of the bell was curvy in its way, but it was still easy enough to read when you were looking at it from a level place: LEWISTON WESTERN STAGE AND RAIL INC. Up high, you could see there were letters there, but it'd be uphill to tell just what they spelled out. I found a fence pole out in back that didn't get used by Mr. Starett and it was about nine feet tall. Salt Springs didn't have many nine-feet-tall people, so that's what I proceeded to use.

Every once in a while, I looked over at Billy while he was finishing up the front door. The door would be the last piece, in a way, the last piece of the whole construction outline. The frame would be up, and you could easy imagine what it was going to look like once the walls got filled in and there was a roof. Billy always worked hard, before Black Iodine and after that, too, and he was working hard now, but it had turned grim and sad now. Used to be he was building a thing that was nothing but good and joy. Now he seemed to be going at it just as hard, but more now because he was there and didn't know how to get himself out. I thought about asking him about that when we broke to at lunch. Decided not to.

Billy and me sat there eating, not saying a word, so quiet that all we could hear was the sounds we made chewing and swallowing, which is gastric ghastly, so I looked up at the sky and said it looked like it might rain, which it didn't, but it was better than the chewing, swallowing serenade.

He looked up at the clouds, took another bite of his hard roll. "You figure to be done getting that bell up by the end of the day?"

So we wasn't going to talk about the rain that

wasn't going to happen. "It'll take you and me and one other to get it into the hole and solid straight."

"I'll see what Heflin's doing tomorrow morning. Maybe he can loan us some gut."

"You figured what you're going to tell Blackthorne and Starett about not stopping by Honey's?"

"Goddammit, Wilbur! Where'd that come from? We were talking about getting Heflin to help out with the bell pole! And then you all of a sudden start talking about Blackthorne and Starett and whatever crap they're layin' out for us! That wasn't what we were talking about, now was it?"

"It wasn't, Billy. You're right about that there."

He gnawed on his hard roll. He didn't want to smile, but couldn't help it. "Now, what in hell were we talkin' about anyway?"

"Finishing up. You be done with the door pretty soon, looks like."

"Three o'clock. Four maybe. Might go over and say hello to Black Iodine a while after."

"How's that working out?"

"We're up to where I can get a little cotton blanket on his back. He'll run around till it blows off, but it's more like a game, seems like. He's not frightened like he used to be."

"Saddle blanket next?"

"Half a saddle blanket maybe. But at least it's some progress. I could use a little progress somewhere along about now." He stood up quick, wiping his hands off on his britches. He moved off toward the schoolhouse. He stopped and turned in a half circle, looking back at me. "I'm sorry I snapped off at you there, Wilbur."

"It happens. Cowboy cussedness. It happens."

"Wilbur, I got to go along with this damned thing Blackthorne and Starett want. I got no choice. If I don't, they'll move my butt out of here and everything I'm trying to put together for me and Pearline just goes up in smoke."

"Billy, Honey doesn't fire up the stove on Sundays. You and Pearline will still have Sundays."

"That's not it. Well, sure, that's part of it, but the main thing is what you told me about why I got this schoolteacher job, that they picked me because I'll be a putty doll to them, doing whatever they want me to do. And the first thing they come out with, what I do, why, I do just what they want me to do, just like they figured would happen all along."

"Billy, you said about things you got planned for you and Pearline. What are those things?"

He smiled, liked thinking on it, sharing it, saying it out to be heard. "Well, if I'm the schoolteacher for the town, that's a weekly amount of salary. That's a steady thing, thing you can use to make plans with. You can save up with a steady thing. Wouldn't be any reason why Pearline couldn't end up walking out of Honey's and her and me settle in together."

"Billy, there is. There is a reason."

"What?"

"Everybody'd know that she used to be a dove at Honey's. That'd make almost everything fracture."

Billy hunkered down slow, picking at the grass stubs, looking away, not seeing anything when he looked. "Tell me something, Wilbur."

"If I can."

"Does there ever come a day when it gets smooth and easy? Does there ever come a day when you open your eyes and look around and know there won't be one scrape or bump or added pain?" His face was a wide-open sunflower.

"That'd be a fine thing, Billy. Myself, I'm still waitin' for that time to come along." What I said put the sun behind a thick cloud.

He straightened up, nodded, and nodded again. He started back in the direction of the schoolhouse frame. After four or five steps, he stopped and just bent forward, hands on both knees, rocking back and forth. He looked beaten. Right then, maybe he was.

"I'm going to see Black Iodine," he said.

I couldn't tell if he was talking about me or not.

It'll shame me to my dying day, so I don't take any pride in admitting what I'm about to admit, but the truth of the matter is that after I pinned that gabooned deputy star on my shirt, I stood in front of the cracked old mirror hanging from

the back door of Starett's bunkhouse and posed
this way and that way and the other for quite a
time. I liked the way it made me look, liked the
way it made me feel, like a man of authority and
admirable prestige. You pin a shiny something
on a man's chest, and he starts to feel he got
turned into a shiny something himself. Explains
a lot if you keep it to the front of some thinking.

When I went on in to the bunkhouse, heading
through to the other door that led out to the
corral, Heflin and Dutch was with some others at
a penny-ante and looked over at me when I
walked past. Might have been my imagination,
but I thought they were looking at me in a different way, a more serious respectful way. Billy was
lying on his bunk, almost covered up with a blanket of books. I stopped there by the end of the
bunk. "You talk to Heflin about giving us a hand
with the bell?"

He shook his head.

"You want me to?"

Another head shake. "We'll do it day after tomorrow."

"What'll we do tomorrow?"

"Just come on out, you'll see." Never took his
eyes off the page of the book propped on his
chest.

"What's tomorrow?"

"The day after today. See you in the morning."
Then he glanced away from the page, looked me
up and down. "Nice badge."

I stood there for a time. I don't mind being insulted, but I hate when something gets said and I don't know whether it's a pat or an ass kick. Billy had looked back to his book so there wasn't any way to prod him, so I just went on my way for the door. Just before I stepped out into the moonlight, I heard Dutch say something to someone behind me.

"You put a pair of spurs on a little lamb, it's going to think it knows how to ride the sheepdog."

Then there was a sound of somebody's laughing.

I still don't really know how long it took me and Geezer to get on into Salt Springs. There was a full moon and normal that pulls me up in spirits, but there was a dark place inside at my center that was spreading like those slimy spreads of oil you could see now on One Legged Indian Crick. I knew there wasn't ever going to be any statues put up to honor Wilbur Moss; when you're named Wilbur Moss, you know that real early. I still wasn't easy where I was, being a laugh-out-loud character, a clown without a tent. They was hard going down all the way. And it wasn't any easier when Billy went to his own dark place and pulled up the covers over his head. When you can't stand up straight, you count on having a pardner to lean on, and when that pardner starts to lean himself at the same time, you begin to tip over, there's neither one of you can hold the other one up. I've seen the ladies at weddings, with tears and with their arms around each other holding tight as tight gets to be. Pardners can't do that. Pardners lean and hold each other up, but when they're both leaning, that's a hard thing to do. Maybe the ladies know more than we do, though they might not know how good it is having a pardner either.

I don't know how long it took me and Geezer to make our way to Salt Springs. The moon was a cold sunlight on the street, and I could hear the piano from inside Rooney's when I tethered out front. I stood there for a time, almost thinking about remounting and heading back to the Starett place, but then I caught a look of my reflection in one of the front windows and saw how the deputy badge was catching the moonlight there on my chest. When you wear a badge on your chest, you can't just remount and go on home. I don't know when that got to be a rule, but I'm dead certain it is, even if no one went to the trouble of writing it down, so I went on up across the porch and into what was waiting there.

It was crowded. It was smoky. It was Rooney's.

I wedged closer to the bar, recognizing a lot of faces, but not that many names. The faces were the oil faces and the railroad faces and I'd seen all of them on the street and at the General Store and livery. We'd nod, not knowing each other, but knowing that was probably on the way. You could stand on the stairs and look down into the crowd and tell who was who. The oil men weren't businessmen, but they made do with their heads and what they knew how to do and find out. There was no holsters, no thick leather gun belts, no boots, no spurs. There was city coats in dark tweed and vests with chains from one pocket over to the other. Not a broad brimmed hat in the bunch, just those domey little Irish derbies. You could see a good many of them had noses the color of raspberry jam, with a little curving half moon across their faces where the narrow derby brim didn't do them any good at all out in the sun. But that's what they wore, that's what they stayed with, because it was a city hat and these were city men.

The railroaders were more used to spit and sweat, but there was still a line carved between them and the cow drivers. They were tough on both sides, but the railroaders had scales and gauges and those measuring telescopes out in their supply yard, and that little difference was enough. The three kinds all moved through Rooney's from the bar to the eating room to the card tables and wheel, like salmon and trout and carp all trying to share one pond that was squeezing them all tight at all sides.

I caught Johnny Kenosha's eye and nodded me an order for a beer, which he commenced to pull right then. I needed that beer more than normal, which is why I wasn't pleased to have a hand grip down on my wrist just when I lifted the schooner to my mouth. I looked over to see that the owner of the hand was brand-new Marshal-Sheriff Willard Ganeel.

Shit on a duck.

"Evening, Willard," I said.

"Marshal."

"Beg pardon?"

"'Marshal'. That's how you call me when we meet up. I'm the marshal. You the deputy. That's how we call each other. Mr. Blackthorne found me a book on lawmen. That's what we need a few words about."

He still had hold of my wrist. It was starting to smart some. "Willard—"

"'Marshal,'" he said, strong and low. He manufactured a smile, so it would look better between us. "And you need to put the beer down and order yourself a cup of coffee."

"I don't see that, Willard."

He tightened on my arm and it came down with the schooner of beer onto the mahogany. "You can't drink on duty," the marshal said.

"According to you, I'm pretty much always on duty."

He nodded slow. "That's the way."

"So, if I understand it all, Willard, this job pays pissant wages and I might get killed doing it and I can't go to Honey's and I can't have a beer, so I can't get fucked and I can't get drunk, all so I have the honor of being your helper."

"Look at it this way, Wilbur. Yeah, you can only

have coffee or water when you're in Rooney's, bur Starett and Blackthorne have set it up with Rooney so that you get to drink for free."

"I get free coffee and free water."

"All you want."

Somebody won at the wheel at the back of the room and a big holler went up. People all over were looking around, standing up on chairs, to see what was going on. I just kept staring at Willard Ganeel. His badge was gold. My badge was silver. Somebody won at the wheel. Somebody lost at the bar. I headed outside.

I was almost to the batwings when I felt a hand on my shoulder. If I came around to find myself looking at Willard, I was going to flatten him, but instead I found myself nose to nose with the doughy face that belonged to Omar. His breath was all hops. To me, that smelled pretty good. "I heard," Omar said. "I know how to help."

"Talk, Omar."

"When you come in here, order yourself a cup of coffee. I'll see you at the bar and come over, order myself a beer. You drink down the coffee as quick as you can. I'll pour you a cupful of beer into it."

"Cup'll be hot, Omar. Beer's going to get warm."

Omar wasn't a big man, but he worked to draw himself up as much as he was able. "Wilbur, when the beer you're gettin' comes free, it don't behoove you much to whine about the temperature not being to your liking."

Well, he was right as right gets to be, and that's what I told him right away. He accepted that, but didn't move off. Acted like there was more needed to be said.

"Omar, is there a problem I don't know about?"

His lower lip bounced a bit. "They're bringing in a doctor. People are going to go to that doctor about ailments and aches and I'll just be a carpenter again. When you know ailments and aches, people treat you with respect. When all you know is hammers and nails and saws, you're pretty much a gray horse, and no more'n that."

"You're the best carpenter we got and everybody knows that. Everybody."

Omar's head bobbled. Eyes welled up. "They're changing it, Wilbur. They're changing the dirt under our feet while we're standing on it."

"They call it progress, Omar."

"Then you won't mind if I shit in your boot and call it butter, will ya?" He knuckle-wiped his nose and teetered off to the bar, hands crammed in his back pockets, head down.

I took in as big a gulp of air as I could manage once I got to the boardwalk out in front of Rooney's. The moon was doing its job and it was quiet as velvet in all directions. I decided to walk around a little, let the chill blow through me. Hell, I was a deputy. If anyone asked, I'd say I was on patrol. Had a sound to it.

There was a little flutter of something moving on the other side of the street, but the moon was coming from the backside there, so it was shadows and softness when I looked over at first. Then I saw what the flutter was and I had to lean in, squint, to put a point on it. It was just a shape at first, a dark form on the sidewalk, till I saw that Nicholas was right there moving along with the shape, one hand reached out and hanging on. It wasn't till that shape went by one of the shop windows that I saw the reflection clear and knew it was Pearline.

It was a long cape she was wearing, with a loose peaked hood she had pulled forward. She hardly made a sound moving down the boardwalk, but her being such a tiny thing, that wasn't a second-thought thing. I moved along the opposite side of the street, staying close to the shadows as I could, making as little scrape and scuffle as I could, though that probably wasn't a crucial thing to do because it was clear wherever Pearline was going, she wanted to get there in the time it takes a bear trap to snap shut, and that hoof was pulled hard forward, like a woman might do when she didn't want anyone seeing her.

She made a turn at the back cross street and kept to her pace. I crossed right after her, still holding on the dark shape of her in the cape with its hood, little Nicholas still knotting his fist into the material of the cape. She stopped at the back door of one of the larger houses and tapped three times on the door. No more than two counts went by before a yellow slash of lantern light spilled out over her and Fergus Blackthorne stepped aside to let the two of them in.

Even though I didn't want to see what I seen and didn't want to be there at all, I turned into a hitching post for the next few ticks. The only place I had to go was the Starett bunkhouse, and Billy might be there and asking questions, and those were questions I didn't want to hear or lie to him about. So there I stood.

Until Nicholas started playing that sweet potato and the soft whistling tune came like a ribbon tossed out there into the darkness of the street and I realized it was time for Wilbur Moss to go home. Slow.

VII

Billy was sound asleep when I got back, and later on, after first light, when my bladder ballooned and I needed to go out back, I looked over at his bunk and it was empty. I guessed he was off doing his courtship with Black Iodine and that was good with me, because I didn't want to look him in the eye. I was afraid he'd see something there that would let him know there was something in the shadows he didn't know about. Sorry I knew about it myself.

There aren't many things I like better than a good sleep, but the time just when night goes and dawn arrives is one of those things. So there I was in the yard, tallywhacker in hand, looking out over the dew shining on the grass, hearing some of the morning doves start their song, feeling the cool move off and the warm blow in. Even better once the sluice gate in my belly opened up and I started to kill some of the poison ivy drop by drop. One corner of the sky was getting smeared with a dusty pink, and one of the good things about an old man peeing slow is that he gets a chance to let these times roll over him like good syrup. There's something to be said for slow peein' and bein'.

I was just tucking my tack hammer back into my britches when I realized I'd been hearing something for a good twenty seconds or so and not really been knowing it, that the sound had a way of stitching itself into the sunrise sounds and didn't seem out of place one little bit. Which held water because the sound I was hearing was the sound of a ringing school bell.

I reined in Geezer when we got to the top of the knob that looked down on the little draw where we'd put up the schoolhouse. There were five people in the framed wall-less construction: Billy and four of the doves from Honey's. They were all seated on one of the benches there, hands in their laps. A couple with their hands tucked into those little furry hand-cuddler deals, all looking at Billy Piper, who was up in front of them. The wind was easy, but it was at my back, so I couldn't make out the words he was saying, though I could hear the melody, hear the bright excitement he was riding on. I'd never seen him so boiling over, like he couldn't get a rein on something inside. Pacing back and forth, arms flying around, a book in one hand, flipping through the pages, pointing at some parts of a rectangular page, then handing the book to one of the doves, letting her take a crack at it, then clapping one hand against the other when she got done. And just at the same time it lit into me that I'd never seen Billy Piper like this before, I came to know I'd never seen Billy Piper teach before either. Never seen the like.

I touched up Geezer and we started on down to the school and Billy and his little Saturday class. There was Pearline, and sitting next to her was the mulatto girl Honey kept saying was from Arabia, and the thick Russian girl next, the one with a name I couldn't pronounce right, the one who'd take cowhands up to her room and close the door and then there'd commence to be the sound of substantial robust ass-slapping coming out from behind that door a while after. I didn't know whose ass was getting slapped, and I wasn't formulating any plans to get behind that particular door and find out. On the other side of the thick Russian girl was Honey herself, hair red as blood, lips just the same, face skin the color of oyster shell turned inside out. Once I saw a drunk slap Honey, and her head just plain disappeared in a cloud of puffy pink. Didn't know if Honey was there to learn something or other or just to keep tabs on her girls. Didn't matter. Surprised to see her there for whatever reason. No sign of Nicholas.

Billy heard Geezer's hoof scratches on the loose shale, and waved us on in with a wide spaniel smile. The doves turned in unison, following his look. Honey and the Russian nodded. Pearline smiled, though the smile was all frayed around the edges. The girl who was supposed to be from Arabia never looked up from her book.

Billy threw his arms wide. "No roof and no walls, but it's a schoolhouse now, Wilbur, and we're just winding up the first class!"

"I heard the bell. Sounded fine."

"How long you think it'll take to get the roof on?"

"End of the week."

He looked back at the doves. "See, ladies? Next week we'll be in the shade of a new roof, so there won't be any excuses about the sunshine making it too hard to do any reading." He gave Honey a little book, putting her in charge of returning it next week and making sure the girls each took time to read up on what was in there, which Honey solemnly promised to do. All the while he was handing out the what-to-do's, I had my eye on Pearline. I couldn't lose that picture of her from last night, gliding along the boardwalk in that long hooded cape, Nicholas gripping on to the material, towed along like a dory behind a two-masted sloop. Then, the lantern light from inside Fergus Blackthorne's place falling across her when he opened the door to let her in. And now, her in the bright sunshine of a new day, sitting there and taking in every word of Billy's, like a baby bird with its mouth open waiting for Momma to get back to the nest. I never got very smart about women, so I didn't know if one was a lie and the other was real, or if they were both branches off the same tree with only one of them getting the light. All I knew solid was that I had something inside me that'd rip Billy Piper apart if I let him know it.

Billy walked the doves off to where Honey had tied off the rig. There were waves and see-ya's, and Honey took hold of the reins like a beer wagon teamster and they rolled off down the road, Billy standing there looking after till they were out of sight, then walking back to me, grinning like never before, which is saying a lot.

"Did you see, Wilbur?"

"I don't know. I was watching for a while from up top there. What was I supposed to see?"

"Me. Me teaching." He looked down at the bench where the doves had been sitting. "They were all listening to me and I was reading to them and they were grabbing on to every word, every blessed one."

"What were you teaching?"

"Reading mostly. Honey and Pearline already got feet under them about that. The Arabian girl can write her name in printing, but not much more than that."

"Billy, she's no more Arabian than—"

"And the Russian girl can't read a lick. She can

read in Russian, she says, but it's all different, because they've got letters in their alphabet we don't even have! Did you ever know that? I never did."

"No. Didn't know it."

"I'll have to look it up somewhere. There's a teachers college in Cody. Maybe I could write out there and they could tell me about that."

"Billy, slow down. You're wearing my ears out."

He laughed, spun around in a circle, almost falling down. "Don't you see, though, Wilbur? Don't you see?"

"Told you. I was up on top there for a while watching."

"No, no. Not that. I actually taught them, Wilbur. They know something now they didn't know when Honey drove the rig on out here! I taught . . . Me, Billy Piper . . . I'm a teacher. I can do it. I can take some little piece of knowing something and hand it over to somebody else and they're not the same somebody else they were when they walked in! Damnit, Wilbur, that's magic. It's just damned powerful magic, is what it is."

"So now you're a schoolteacher."

His head bobbed. He spun in the direction of the framed skeleton we put up. "I thought I could make up a little place in the back there. A two-room something where Pearline and I could start off when the time was right. Schoolteacher can't live in a ranch bunkhouse anyway."

"You figure you and Pearline gonna tie it up?"

"Sure." He saw the look on my face. "Why not?"

"Billy, everyone's gonna know what Pearline used to do, what she used to be. It's one thing behind doors at Honey's. It's another when we're talking about the wife of the schoolteacher. Shit on a duck, you must know that."

"When me and Pearline tie up, she won't be doin' that anymore."

I hated poking holes in him, but couldn't seem to stop. "Billy, folks will know. They won't forget."

"Wilbur, these people comin' in are churchgoers. Churchgoers are supposed to forgive."

"Churchgoers are supposed to do a lot of things churchgoers never get around to doing, and we both know that."

The look he gave me was level and strong. He walked across the new flooring, the limp of his making a tempo you couldn't sing to. He stopped next to Geezer, reached up, and wrapped his hand light around the horn on my saddle. "Wilbur," he said, "it doesn't matter about the floor you're scrubbing. What matters is the dream you're dreaming when you're scrubbing that floor."

"And you and Pearline got dreams."

"We do."

I felt like a pack mule getting more loaded on than he could take. I jerked my head off in the direction of the road. "I haven't had breakfast yet. Going to go see what Cookie's scraped off the floor." I pulled Geezer's head around and moved off for the road.

"Wilbur!" Billy Piper called. "Didn't you ever have yourself a dream?"

I pulled Geezer's head up, turned back in Billy's direction.

"I know it was probably a buncha years ago," he said. "But there had to be a time when you had some kinda dream kicking you in the butt."

I had an answer, but it wasn't an answer I could easy give out with, because it had to do with family, and the only family I had right now was all under the roof of Starett's bunkhouse, and Billy was central to that and he was tilting to move out the door. I could straighten that tilt up if I told him where Honey was sending Pearline at nights now, but that'd break something inside him, and I'd spent too much time in Black-thorne's barn getting him back together to ever rip him apart like that. So, I said: "Yeah, I had me a dream once. It had to do with me having a horse cock and a harem!"

He busted out at that, the laugh high-pitched and open. He was laughing more now than at any time since I'd knowed him.

I been around enough gasping gurglers to know that dying is a hard thing to do, and I was coming to find that trying to die is pretty near to impossible. I don't mean swallowing a Colt barrel and letting fly; I mean where you talk in your head and decide that if everything stopped while you were sleeping and you woke up dead, you might not think it was the worst day of your life. That's what was going through me when my head hit the rope mattress that night. I was trying to move forward, which is what life is when you get down to it, but every step I started to think about was into steam or ice and there wasn't any going forward at all. So I closed my eyes and told myself I'd just stop sometime during the night and see what darkness is and whether or not there's peace there.

Which got me a really good night's sleep and let me wake up as rested as I think I've ever been, except for those times I've humped myself to a stupefied state. When I rolled up to a sit and looked around, I saw the bunkhouse was empty except for Heflin standing at the window, using the reflection there to help him with the morning shave. He heard me grunt coming off the bunk, and nodded. "Morning."

"If you say so." I stretched out, scratched my bottom. It was well past first light. Apparently that trying-to-die-stuff really works. "Where is everybody?"

"Out to the ridge pasture. I was out there myself. Had to come back for the water wagon."

"And to scrape off some whiskers."

"They grow when I'm on wages. They can get

scraped off the same time." He started working on the little valley right under his nose.

"What're they doing out at the ridge pasture?"

He didn't answer for a time. It was delicate work where he was scraping. "Culling out the ones who won't get through the drive."

"The drive? They big enough so soon?"

"You been busy, Wilbur. You been working on the schoolhouse with Billy and all that. We decided we'd keep on feeding the beeves even if you was there to supervise and tell us all what we were doing wrong. I guess we got lucky; they kept gettin' heft on 'em even without you looking on."

There it was, the way out of all the pincers squeezing me from every side. The notion of the drive, the time out on the move, the night sky and the stink and the sweat and the moaning beasts all around, that would get me out from under. Bless Heflin. He showed me the light. "When do we leave?"

"There ain't no 'we' about this, Wilbur. You ain't goin'."

"What the hell are you talking about? If there's a drive, I'm going on the drive. I always go on the drive."

Hef sopped a rag in the water, started to wipe off his face. "Starett and Fergus Blackthorne say different."

"How come? Who talked to them?"

"I did. Asked if you was still on the ranch as a hand and they both said no. Said you were a city employee now. You are Willard's deputy, they both said." He checked on his reflection a little more, then dropped the wet towel on the sill. He turned away from the window for the first time, looked at me straight on. "I guess you must be doin' a good job."

"I ain't doin' any job at all, dammit. Haven't stopped a fight. Haven't arrested a soul."

"Looks like you got all the bad boys intimidated, Wilbur."

I was still in my raggedy long johns and no shoes. Not very intimidating or impressive-looking. I musta looked like a beggar on the street corner. I held out both hands palm up in Hef's direction. "Hef, Hef . . . Don't do this to me. I'm a hand. You know I'm a hand. I need to get out on the trail, Hef. I need that more'n I ever needed anything, Hef. I never been bumpin' you for favors. I never asked for a soft ride. Tell Fergus, tell Starett. Tell 'em you need me out there."

"Wilbur, they were pretty tied down about this. They were both bone hard about it. Besides, if I was you, I'd be looking forward to sticking around here. It looks like it's going to be about as interesting a time as this town's ever seen."

"Jesus, Hef, stop. I heard all the sermons about the future with the railroad and the oil and all that's going to come to be."

"I was thinking more about Pearline and Fergus."

I know my heart kept pumping, and I know I

kept taking air in, blowing it out, but it seemed like everything just froze up. Like sometimes, even a waterfall will freeze up, a solid ice wall with ripples and waves solid as stone. That's how I felt after Hef said what he said. Frozen waterfall, spring nowhere in sight.

Hef saw me, knew me well enough to know. "Wilbur . . . There a snag somewhere?"

"The thing about Pearline and Fergus. Where'd you hear it?"

"Rooney's."

"Who from?"

"Honey. She was drinking. Thought it was funny. Fergus laying out a bogus on Honey with the city employees, then calling her about some sheet warmer over at his place on nights when the wick got warm."

Shit on a duck. If it got said at Rooney's, it got said all over Salt Springs before there was another sunset. "Any of the other boys there?"

"Whole bunch."

If you was walking on a trail and came across a burning fuse, you might decide to turn tail and get the hell outta there as quick as you can. You might not need to see a dynamite stick at all; some things you just assume. Some things go together in your head quick as spit. That's what it was with Honey talking her talk in Rooney's; it was going to get back to Billy and sooner than later. Some things you just assume. You don't always have to see the damned dynamite stick.

"Wilbur, the boys know better than to say anything to Billy."

Which I knew was so. None of the boys under Starett's roof ever put in a call for Pearline when they went to Honey's. I don't recollect anybody ever talking about it; it was just something we all knew was a right way to go. We might beat the pulp out of each other after a game of penny-ante, might kick a nut off if one poke crossed another. That was all the way. But the notion of leaving our spend in a woman another poke valued true was not in anybody's kit.

But Billy would find out, and he'd ask if I knew, and it wouldn't ever be the same between me and my pal again, not ever.

I got out to the schoolhouse about an hour later and Billy was there, working on the back wall. All the lumber for the roof was there by now, and he had dragged out the ladder from Starett's barn to get ready for putting a hat on his castle. I got the ladder up against the side and started carrying the boards on up, one at a time. Billy offered to help me, talking about setting up a pulley to move things quicker, but I waved him off, lying that I had my own way of doing things when it came to a roof, which was bald-faced balderdash, but it kept him and me working in different places and that was good, because I couldn't grab on to it any other way. After a while, I was sweating like a sausage on the griddle and my shirt couldn't get any blacker, so

I came on down to get some water. I took a long pull and let the coolness slip down and heard the grass next to me crinkle when Billy sat himself down next to me. I held out the canteen and he took it. No talking for a little while. We just puffed there in the summer sun.

"Coupla the girls told Pearline they liked the class," he said.

"When'd you see Pearline?"

"We walked out this morning, down by One Legged Indian Crick."

"And they liked it, huh?"

"That's what they told Pearline. Especially the Arabian."

"Billy, she's no more Arabian than I'm a Choctaw."

"Going to take her at her word, Wilbur. Not my place to call someone out as a liar just because there's questions floating around. She wants to be Arabian, then I'll call her Arabian. Don't hurt me and might help something for her."

I sometimes forgot how young Billy Piper was. Stupid and young aren't the same thing, but God knows they're next-door first cousins. "Nicholas wasn't at your class," I said.

"He's young. Honey wanted him to sleep in. Said he was up late the night before. Some kinda goings-on at Honey's."

Billy and me once had a long campfire talk about how hard it's got to be to be a doctor when you have to lay out something awful for one of your patients. What words do you use, what pillow can you find to wrap around those words? I remember feeling sorry for the made-up doctor we was talking about, but no more. That damned doctor knew what he was getting in to when he decided he'd be a doctor, so he couldn't claim to be surprised when the casket in the next room needed to be explained. But all that was in the pot when he sat down to play. He wasn't handed that duty on account of being happenstance on the boardwalk out in front of Rooney's seeing a thing that would tear his pardner up like a straight razor back and forth slap. "Well," I said, "I bet Nicholas will like class. Hc's a bright one."

"He went out playing with me and Pearline Sunday. He was off his feed. Hardly played that sweet potato at all."

"Well, like you said, things getting busy all over at Honey's, sounds like."

"I wouldn't know," Billy said.

"Me neither, Billy. Me neither. I was just saying that because that's what you told me. You and me are in the same boat as far as going to Honey's goes."

"Don't think that's exactly true, Wilbur." He was looking straight out, treetop level. It was an older face than usual for Billy.

"Oh, I know that. I know you got Pearline and I'm just a stump jumper. I just meant as far as going to Honey's is all I meant. I didn't mean to

say it was just the same with you and me. We're
not twinned up or anything like that."

"You ever loved a woman deep, Wilbur?
Hurtin' deep?"

And shit on a duck, there was an explosion in
my skull like someone was hammering a nail into
me. A flood of pictures came whipping through
me, mostly forgettable sweatables I been with
over the times, but one kept pushing through,
and her hair was red and her name was Alma
and her and me wrapped around each other
after a dance at Fort Phil Kearney. Her pap was
the sergeant major there, and I was working
breaking horses for the new troop coming in,
and afterwards she stroked the back of my neck
where we lying out under the willows, and she
told me about her thinking on life and what she
thought it would hold for her. Her voice was a
whisper, and I remember thinking I never knew
a time in my life when I was more easy and at
home with everything. I never saw skin as pale
white as her breasts, and her thighs was what
clouds must be made of, if clouds could be made
of something like silk. Alma was her name, and I
hadn't a thought of Alma in ten turtle lifetimes,
until Billy had asked me about loving a woman
deep. I guess I did once, but I forgot to tell her.

Billy said: "You're going to give me an answer
or not?"

"Not," I said and got up, climbed the ladder,
and started to work on the roof. I could feel his

eyes watching me. Hell, I could feel me watching me. Alma's last name was Poindexter.

"Starett loves his wife deep," Billy called up.

"He does."

"You think Fergus Blackthorne ever loved his wife that way?"

He was picking at a wound he couldn't see, but I could feel it right to the core. "We come here to build a schoolhouse, or to prattle like a buncha old ladies at a play party?"

He got most of the side wall up and I got a bunch done on the roof.

I had half a mind to ride on into Rooney's and half a mind is what that notion came from, being as I was making Rooney's more of a habit than it ought to be. Billy grabbed himself a couple apples off of Cookie's shelf, so I figured he was heading over to feed Black Iodine and smooth him out a touch. I wondered if Fergus ever saw Billy out at the corral. If he ever walked out to talk with Billy, see what he was up to, wondered what Billy would do if he ever heard from Fergus about Pearline's stopping by. I don't know total what cowboys are good for or good at, but I do know that wondering wasn't one of them. I swung over to the bunkhouse.

There was a game of mumblety-peg going on over in the corner, with Heflin's pigsticker being used by five or six of the boys, Heflin looking on with pride, like he was the parent, not the owner. The Dutchman had his scripture book out, which probably meant he was headed for Rooney's, then Honey's, knowing all he had to do was pray how wrong he'd been after he got back and forgiveness was in the mail. He looked up when I walked past him and he smiled, and I knew that meant trouble. He was up on his feet moving behind me before I even got to my bunk. When my butt hit the blanket, there he was looking down.

"Rode out past the schoolhouse yesterday. Lookin' fine, I think."

"We're making progress."

"You and Billy working on it together, is that how it goes?"

"That's how it goes."

"And how is old Billy?" Him using "old" was like Miz Starett saying "shit." Didn't fit.

"I guess he's doing fine."

"He's a nice kid. I worry about him."

"You worry about Billy?"

"I do."

"When did that start? I don't recollect you worrying much about anybody, Dutchman."

The Dutchman made a noise that was supposed to be a chuckle, but a frog gets closer to whistling than he did to laughing. "Oh, I don't say out my feelings much, but I care about people, worry about people. Just like I know a lot of people worry about me, even if they don't speak it out."

"You know that people worry about you."

"I do."

"What people would that be?"

"You, Wilbur."

"Me? I worry about you?"

"Wouldn't come as a surprise."

"And why should I worry about you, Dutchman?" I started to realize I wasn't hearing Heflin's pigsticker go thumping into the floorboards like before. The mumblety-peggers were all looking over to where the Dutchman and I were talking.

Dutch sat on the bunk next to mine. He held out both hands, a beggar's message. "Because I was thinking on going in to town and stopping at Rooney's and then taking myself over to Honey's, but I looked in my poke and I miscalculated my funds, Wilbur. I don't have enough to afford to make that plan real."

"Sad story, Dutchman. Not sure it's the first time it ever happened in this world."

He went on like I hadn't said a whisper. "And I was thinking to myself: 'If Wilbur knew I had this situation, he might reach into his pocket and do a rightness to help me out some.'"

"That's what you thought." Somebody in the mumblety-peg bunch laughed low.

The Dutchman's head moved up and down real slow. "And then I thought: 'And if Wilbur won't help me out, maybe I'll go look up Billy Piper and tell what I got in mind,' though that's not what I'd prefer to do, because there's always a chance I might slip up and mention something about Pearline paying nighttime good-time visits to Fergus Blackthorne's. I wouldn't want to do that, understand, but you know how it is with us who don't speak English from our birthdays. Sometimes, the words come out in ways we hardly understand ourselves."

There's a cross-eyed kinda power that comes to me at times like this one was, because what takes power away from us is not knowing what's around the corner, what noon's going to be like while we're standing there at dawn. Because I knew what was coming next; I could see a little way into the future, and that's better than most times are, even if the future you're knowing about involves an old windbreak like Wilbur Moss getting the puddin' kicked out of his nut sack. The Dutchman and me looked at each other for a little while. Didn't see that there was much to be gained by drawing it out. I shifted my weight a little, then rolled backwards as hard as I could, throwing my right leg out stiff. I hoped the toe of my boot would catch him under the chin, but I guess he flinched back a hair, because it was the boot heel that made contact, though it was flush on it. The kick got his tongue to get caught between his teeth, and by the time I rolled up on the other side of my bunk, there was a generous spurt coming out from between his lips and the lower half of his face was looking like he had a scarlet neckerchief wrapped around him. His voice was more buffalo than man and his eyes were uncordial.

The Dutchman launched himself across

the bunk and the top of his head hammered hard into my gut, and I heard myself pig-grunt and tasted something at the back of my throat I had called breakfast just a while back. Then God come down out of the sky and decided to give the Dutchman four more pairs of hands, and he started using each and every one of them to turn this wincing old man into something you'd throw over the back of a couch. I knew the other boys would jump in and pull the Dutchman off me because I'm old and rheumy and he's bear mean as it gets, and as soon as I knew they'd pull him off, I knew I was wronger than ever. And it started getting dark then, with the every once in a while sparkle of lightning going off way behind my eyes. No thunder.

For the first time in my life, I wasn't squiffed when I had my head deep in the water at the horse trough. I lifted my head out, spitted some, sputtered some more, and when the throbbing took over the cabin I called my head, I poked myself back down into the coolness. I stayed there as long as I could, opened my eyes, and damned near died of the apoplexy when I found myself looking into two dark holes and two pool-ball-sized eyes right opposite mine. I screamed like a stuck pig and yanked back.

I butt-crawled back from the trough, then opened up my eyes and saw Geezer standing on the other side of the trough. There was a curtain of slobber water coming down off his mouth. He wasn't pretty dry; wet, he could curdle a prune.

"How's your breath?"

Heflin was sitting on the rail. The stink from the turd-length thing he was smoking fit well with how I was feeling. He took in a puff, blew out a straight gray plume. "How's your breath, I said."

I put my hands on my ribs, took in a quick gasp. Hurt some, didn't scorch my insides. "Tolerable."

"He worked on your gut for quite a time. Wanted to make sure you weren't busted."

"You coulda made sure of that by stepping in."

"I wanted to, Wilbur. I was even taking steps in that direction. But I had a knife in my hand, and that move could have set things off in the wrong way and nobody would want that. Even you wouldn't want that."

"Why 'even' me?"

"On account of you being a deputy." Long puff on the stogie fouled things a bit more. "What do they call it? A higher standard."

"Hef, you're a no-good sonofabitch."

"Actually, I'm a very good sonofabitch. Had a whole lifetime practicing up to get good at it." He nipped off the glowing end of his cigar, scraped away at the warm gray, tossed it on the ground. Geezer's head swept low, and he roamed back and forth over it for a tick, then started to chew away on the black sour root. I wouldn't want to be walking behind Geezer tomorrow.

"Where'd the Dutchman go?" I said.

"Into town, I expect."

I reached my hand around to my butt pocket, pulled out my bandanna. I unknotted it, spread it flat on the dirt. Everything was still there, every cent, every dollar. I looked up at Hef. "He didn't take my money."

"I stopped him. You're welcome."

"So the Dutchman went into town without my money?"

"Seems the case."

"You think he'll go looking for Billy?"

"Wilbur, how can I know what a crazy old carbuncle like the Dutchman might do? He might go do any old thing at all."

There's people in this world, men mostly from what I've seen, who cannot abide something that's straightforward and honest and good. They don't even abide the word "good" itself. If a thing is tough and smelly and a little bit scarred up, they'll buy it a drink and a ticket to the baths. But if a thing or a person had some care and innocence about the edges, they had to find a way to get it scuffed up the very best they could. I think if there's enough people in line at the table, there'll always be somebody needs to spit in the soup. Heflin was one of those people. I stood up slow, joints popping like a Mexican dancer's little clickers. My lip was swole up and there was a draining slit at the edge of my mouth. I owed the Dutchman for all a that. I started moving for Geezer.

"Where you off to, Wilbur?"

"You know where I'm off to. I'm off to town."

"Gonna teach that goddamned Dutchman a lesson, huh?"

I had to grab under my knee to lift my leg high enough to foot the stirrup. I grabbed on to the horn and took in a deep gulp. Closed my eyes and pulled myself onto the saddle. My head hurt, wobbled a bit inside. When it all settled, I looked down, and Heflin was standing there next to Geezer, a needling smile in place.

"You sure you're up to riding into town, Wilbur? You look a little wrung out."

"I'm fine."

"I was going to hang some banner flags out. You could stay here, help me out."

He wasn't making a lick of sense. "Banner flags? What are you talking about banner flags for?"

"Hell, Wilbur. Look at the calendar. In a week, it's going to be the Fourth of July. You know how Fergus Blackthorne is about the Fourth of July. And Starett goes right along with him on it."

"Fergus is going to go through all that whoop 'n' holler even though his wife's gone? She was the reason for all that, I thought."

"Well, Wilbur, maybe Fergus Blackthorne has

gone and got himself a brand new reason." He grinned wide. He was a happy cowboy.

I touched up Geezer, and we moved out of the dooryard and onto the road to Salt Springs. About halfway into town, I tried to think of something I should have said to Heflin. It would be something really smart and tough and sharp.

I was tying off in front of Rooney's when it came to me. I just stopped moving, staring out into the very last flare of the sunset. I didn't want to move because it seemed to me like the idea was so near perfect, so new baby with all toes and fingers, that I could barely make myself think it through I was that fearful of finding a crack. But there wasn't any. I had the idea that was going to get me out from under. I was going to go in to Rooney's wearing my deputy badge and start me a fight. I was going to find some bloomer butt and pick on him and swing hard, and they'd have to rip that deputy badge off my chest with both hands. And if I wasn't deputy, there'd be no reason why I couldn't be out on the trail drive, and I'd be shed of Salt Springs by the time Billy found out about Fergus Blackthorne and Pearline's nighttime visitations. I wouldn't be there to help him, that was true, but I didn't see what help I had to give anyway and I didn't want to be there to see it all, because what is also true is that when a man gets a lot of rings around the trunk, he wants to dodge away from pain, his most of all, and what Billy was facing would pain me hard. I opened up the saddlebag and pulled out the deputy badge. Pinned it on as straight as the schoolhouse roofline and moved to the Rooney batwings.

I held up just inside, looking around for anyone soft around the gut who showed signs of being in Rooney's for most of the night. Nobody lean, mean, and eager for Wilbur Moss. Then I saw him sitting at the chuck-a-luck table. Fringy hair and wearing a tight suit coat with a fake flower in the buttonhole. Didn't know who he was, but the pasty face pretty much was a guarantee that he was one of the mining engineers, and they most struggle with knuckles to the nose, it's been said. And besides, I wasn't on the lookout for a donnybrook, just enough of a nosebleed to get me fired off the force. Shouldn't take much.

"Wilbur, what the dickens happened to you?" The voice belonged to Willard Ganeel, and he was standing right next to me, looking worried.

"Nothing happened to me, Willard. Why?"

"Don't lie to me, Wilbur. Your face looks like somebody tried to take out a tooth while your mouth was shut tight." He moved closer and his voice got secret soft. "Is somebody trying to intimidate you, Deputy?"

"Oh, Willard . . ."

He put his hand on my shoulder and turned me off to the side, away from the chuck-a-luck table and the little pasty-faced target I had picked out. I smelled flowers, and looked around before I realized Marshal Willard Ganeel had discovered Sweet Lilac Cologne. "Because I've heard about the lawmen being intimidated by bulldog bullyboys who think the law doesn't apply to them. And I won't have that in Salt Springs, not with all the new things in our future."

"Willard, so help me, no one's tryin' to—"

"Then tell me how your face got all puffed up. Tell me how come you got that new cut on your mouth? Tell me that."

Hard to know how a man could smell like flowers and still manage to talk like shit, but Willard seemed to have the knack. I did as much thinking as I could. "Willard, this is between you and me, okay? This doesn't go a step beyond you and me."

He liked that; it sounded like someone might have to swear on something or take an oath. "I'm the marshal, Wilbur. Who can you trust if you can't trust the appointed law?"

It was a good question, but I decided to stay on the topic. "Willard, you know Honey's?"

He looked to see if there was anyone close. "Yeah. I guess I know Honey's."

"You know about the Russian girl at Honey's?" Willard got bulgy-eyed. "Well, I've heard some."

I pointed my finger toward my face. "She'll sell you a special ticket for this," I said.

There was a gap opened between Willard's lips about four nickels' worth. "I didn't know that."

"Not many do." The gap between Willard's lips

was staying there, so I took a peek back over my shoulder to where Mr. Pastyface had been sitting at the chuck-a-luck. There was no luck; he was gone. I went back to Willard. "You seen Billy Piper tonight, Marshal?"

It took him a while to erase the blackboard and move on. "Yeah. Yeah, I did."

"Where was he?"

"He was at the bar having a beer with the Dutchman."

"The Dutchman? A beer with the Dutchman?"

"I think the Dutchman was buying."

I felt somebody put a mountain on my shoulders, and I sunk back against the wall. Eventually, I guess every ship sinks. "You see which way he went when he left?"

"Did not. And, Wilbur, about the Russian girl. You're not supposed to be going into Honey's at all."

I locked eyes with him and stood up straight. I put my hands on his shoulders. I couldn't say how far apart our noses were, but I could smell the lilacs. "Willard," I said, "I just told you about the Russian girl and me. And to talk back the talk you talked to me, who can I trust if I can't trust the appointed law?"

Willard took that in solemn, and then he nodded once. He stepped back. I let my hands fall to my sides and almost tilted a formal bow to him, took a step straight back, and then turned around and walked out through the door and let a lot drain out of me when I got to the porch outside Rooney's. The mountain on my shoulders was gone. Then it was back.

There was that velvet hooded cape moving down the boardwalk like a ship slipping through the shallows. Nicholas was the ferry towed along behind, fist tight in the velvet, his head down. I watched them till they swung around the corner and moved down the street that led to the back door of the place where Fergus Blackthorne was. A little flutter of movement took my eye farther down the street, and I saw I wasn't the only one watching that passage. There was a tall figure next to the livery stable, but the moon was low and I couldn't make out who I was looking at. All I could see was that the tall figure didn't move, just stood watching Pearline and Nicholas for a long time, watching and not moving for a long time. Then I heard the door at the back of Fergus Blackthorne's place open and, a tick or two later, close up tight, with the bolt thrown hard. Then the tall figure by the livery stable moved out into the street and started away.

The tall figure had himself a sizable limp.

I didn't go back to the Starett ranch that night. A part of me was easy about that on account of what I saw, but that wasn't the reason I stayed in Salt Springs. The reason there was the bubbling gurgle that was coming from Geezer's gut. I figured the reason was the cigar of Heflin's that got gobbled down a few hours earlier. I couldn't say certain what the effect on old Geezer might be, but I knew I didn't want to be close to Geezer when it was time to find out, whether front end or back. So I stored Geezer in the livery stable corral and I pooched up a buncha straw in the barn, tried to go to sleep there. Didn't have much accomplishment when it came to the sleeping part, though. Hardly any at all.

It was soft mother-of-pearl all across the sky when I came out of the barn. When I moved around to Geezer in the corral, the mother-of-pearl was overtook by the stench of horse crap and Lord knows what else had been spewed out during the night. I got me a bucket and filled it up from the trough, cleaned up what I could, but I still didn't have much faith that Geezer was certified safe for the ride out to the schoolhouse, so I headed out on my own, leaving Shit Flanks looking after me with a curious look.

Rooney's was just cracking the doors wide when I walked in. Not like me to go there this early looking for a drink, but I already resolved to spend this whole day getting lost in any way I could. It was a day I was going to start out by having more to drink than a sane man ought to have before noon, but being sane wasn't very close to the top of the list of things I wanted to happen today. My belly was tomb empty, so there was a sizable effect taking place after the third dose of Dr. Whiskey. I was breathing open-mouthed and sweating more'n the temperature called for. Cicero tried to turn deaf when I asked for a bottle to take with, but I wore him down and walked out with it under my arm half an hour later.

I didn't like walking out to the schoolhouse because it meant being afoot, and there's something unmanly about that to my way of thinking. There's a power comes from the saddle, from being up high and feeling all that muscle under you willing to do what you tell it to do. And while I still think that to the core, I have to say that thinking comes more easy to a walking man than one with leather under his backside. Maybe it's the smell or the dirt, the stone crunch you can feel under the boot heel, or maybe it's just that a man's smaller when he walks and being small makes him afraid and fear leads to thinking. I'm not sure about any of that. I'm just sure that a walking man thinks more.

My thinking was that the boil was red for a time, and now it was turning mealworm white and had to pop itself pretty soon now. I didn't want to be around to see it, but there didn't appear to be any train coming through that had a ticket with Wilbur Moss's name on it. It was going to end bad, there was no question about. It was going to end bad and Wilbur Moss was a hobbled gelding, useless and sad and empty.

When I come to the clearing, my shirt was

soaked black and sticky, but when I saw the schoolhouse framed like it was, none of that was important. You could see what the place was going to look like, see that more than likely we'd be looking to paint in a week or ten days. Billy had done some more work on the back wall, and the tall pole where we'd put the bell was wrapped with red, white, and blue bunting. I'm not any kind of flag waver or parader, but for a little tick, something boomed up inside me, until I recollected that Fergus Blackthorne had put a sizable brand on the day and most folks thought it was more his than theirs.

I uncorked my glass compadre and took a pull before I put the ladder up and had a foot on the first rung. Not much of a secret that roof work and barley breakfast have some shortcomings, but fact is, I didn't give sand about that. I'd started out to get lost and whiskey can do that, just like hard work can. I'm a man, and men have skills when it comes to finding ways to hide. I started to climb on up.

The sun was quartered high now, and the heat didn't come from just the bottle anymore. I lined the boards proper, for a man with some shining inside, and took my time to make sure the nailing was flush and constant. I wasn't one to carry a watch, couldn't afford to, and wouldn't if I could. Watching time is having time run you, insteada you running time the way you want. So, I don't know how long I was up there, nose to the boards, taking my sips, doing a good job on the roof and listening to everything that was in that pus boil that was ready to roar. But it was getting hotter and I was beginning to lose some spine. I emptied out what I had, spilled it down my throat, then rolled over on my back on the slant there and started to close my eyes. Then, somebody in my skull started to wave a red flag about that, so I did something out of step for me, which was that I actually went and did something smart. I grabbed on to the hammer and snatched up some nails, rolled over, and bunched up some of the material of my sopping shirt sleeve, and hammered the nail through the cloth on one side, then scrunched as much as I could and nailed down another part of the shirt material farther down. Me in the shirt, shirt nailed solid to the roof boards. I took the arm that wasn't nailed to the roof and tilted my hat down over my face, and then I just let it all settle inside, melted away every hard part I still was carrying around, and I don't think I've ever been so syrup soft in my life, at least not since they lifted me out of the crib. I could hear my breathing slow, and even my heart sounded more gentled down. It was dark under the hat, and I needed the dark more than anything, and I remember thinking to pin a medal on my soul because I'd set out to lose Wilbur Moss from Wilbur Mos and I think I got there a lot sooner than even I thought.

After a time, Alma was there. She was riding

Geezer through a rolling meadow, the grass tall and whipping back and forth, little ribbons cutting across the stalks. Alma didn't have a stitch on top, just a froth of a light blue skirt, and her breasts swayed soft with Geezer's pace. She sat Geezer like a man would, legs spread wide, thighs outlined under the skirt's veil, hands taloned in Geezer's mane. Alma was smiling.

"Goddamnit, Pearline! Goddamnit-goddamnit-goddamnit!"

I squeezed my eyes tight shut. Alma didn't want to hear a harsh thing like that, not at a sweet time like her and me were having. We had a carve-out place for just the two of us, and there was no call for anything like what got yelled far off in the back of my head. No call.

"But Billy, for years you've been able to—"

"It wasn't Fergus Blackthorne, goddamnit! It wasn't Fergus Blackthorne."

The sun poked in under the edges of my hat. Alma wasn't there anymore, and I had myself nailed down on top of the roof of the new schoolhouse. I could hear walking steps below me, along with a woman crying, mostly the way a scared little kid might cry. I tried to sit up. Couldn't.

"And do you think that was easy? Do you think that was an easy thing for me to do?" Billy's voice was high, close to shredding away.

"No, no, no. I know it wasn't easy. But we were doing it, Billy. We were staying close, weren't we?"

"Goddamnit!"

"Billy, don't. I get scared when you get like this. I know it's hard for you. It's hard for both of us. But we've stayed close. We still talk about our plans, our places we're going to go, places where no one knows what went before. And because we still talk about the plans, I know we both still want the plans to be so. Don't you still want the plans to be so, Billy?"

Footsteps, boot steps, Billy walking to the other side of the frame floor. Only birdsongs after that, and the wind stroking the leaves against themselves.

"Billy, please say something. Please, please, please, say something." Pearline blew her nose.

I started to move, but I was afraid of a board creak. I lay still. I guess I breathed, because I didn't die. I lay still.

"Pearline," he said after a time, "ever since we talked and been together, I loved you more than my next breath. You were so much in my thinking, I couldn't get coffee with cream without I rhymed in my head with your name. And that's crazy, and maybe I was, and maybe that's what love is, or what it does. Hell, I don't know. Maybe nobody knows. But we're in a situation, you and me, we're in a situation hardly anybody's ever been in before, at least not in Salt Springs. And we handled it. Wasn't easy, but we handled it, didn't we?"

"And we can still, Billy. Please let's go on with each other. If a person does a thing, they can keep right on doing it. Please don't give us up. Please, please." I couldn't see her, but I knew the hands were prayerful.

"It's different now."

"Why? Why is it different?" Right on the edge of the tears taking over.

I was feeling a building need to pee. Clench it out. Below was the sound of boot heels. A wood creak as Billy sat down by her. On a church organ, Billy's voice woulda come from the far left-hand side of the keyboard.

"We got by, Pearline, after the boys in Starett's bunkhouse agreed silent not to ask Honey for you when they come in. That let me keep looking straight ahead without pictures getting behind my eyes that turned me inside out. It was plain. There was a door in my mind I never opened, and as long as I didn't open it, we could be together and our plans would be as bright and new as ever they were. Those plans were a door I could open and lean on."

"That can still be so, darlin'. Nothin's changed for us."

Billy's voice stood tall. "Yes, it has, damnit! It's all changed! It's me lying in bed at night and knowing you're lying with Fergus Blackthorne!"

"Stop it! Stop it!"

"I can't stop it! I'd like to! God knows I'd like to! But it's there! It's in my head! I keep seeing him with you, keep seeing him reaching out to touch you soft and—"

There was the sound of a hand slap, like a black-snake whip crack meeting up with a gunshot.

The wind still moved the leaves. A bird called. Another one answered the first. Wilbur Moss lay there on the schoolhouse roof like a butterfly in a collector's case.

"Billy, please don't say anymore. I don't want to talk about this anymore. Let's go back to town."

"You don't want to talk about this anymore."

"No."

"Can't say as I blame you, Pearline."

"Billy—"

"If I was you, I wouldn't want to talk about it either! If I was you, I'd do anything I could to keep from talking about having Fergus Black-thorne be stroking and touching—"

"Stop it, you sonofabitch! Stop it this instant!"

"Why? Why the hell should I?"

"Because I'm not the one Fergus Blackthorne is touching!" Her speaking voice turned to a wail. It didn't come from a high place, like a girl's, but from a deeper place, from a low place.

A long time went by before Billy said a word. "What's that mean . . . you're not the one Fergus is touching? What's that mean?"

"Just what it says, just what it says."

"Pearline, you got to make some sense at least. You're there. Fergus is there."

"Well, that's not so, is it." She let out a long sigh, close to a moan.

I didn't have to be seeing her to know she was rocking back and forth.

"Pearline, you're still not talking sense."

"Billy, oh, Billy."

"What?"

"Use your head, teacher! There's Nicholas! Don't you see? There's Nicholas! There's Nicholas! There's Nicholas!"

"Pearline, Nicholas is a *boy*."

Age isn't about years and knowledge isn't about what you get out of a book on the shelf, and I had just flat out forgotten how young Billy Piper really was. He knew about men who wanted to be on men on account of that drive when we found out about Morrison and Guettner. Shit on a duck. I remember talking to Billy after we packed those two up and sent them on their way, and how he took it in as well as he could, but still couldn't wrap all the way around what they were doing. If that was uphill and slippery for him, Lord knows what the news about Nicholas might be doing.

"Billy, there's men who like boys."

"For that?"

"For that."

"But how?"

And so Pearline told him, told him what went where and who was getting a penetration and who was doing the penetrating. She told it like you'd explain a color to a blind man or a song to the deaf. After a time, I could hear Billy start to whisper soft little "Nos" and "Aw, Gods" into the silent parts.

"Does it hurt him?" Billy said.

"Nicholas, you mean?"

"Nicholas, yeah."

"It does both ways."

"Both ways. What's that mean, both ways?"

"There's a body part hurt. And there's a deeper hurt. Next time you're around Nicholas, just look into his eyes deep as you can. Just look in his eyes, Billy. You'll see what I mean."

"Pearline, I'll tell you something."

"What's that?"

"Fergus Blackthorne's a man who needs to be dead."

"Billy!"

"It's so and you know it's so. A man who'd do that to a child, who'd cut him and scar him inside like that, doesn't deserve one more breath than he's been given already! You know what I'm going to do? I'm going to the damned sheriff or marshal or whatever it is they're calling him now and I'm going to tell him what's got to be done to that sonofabitch! And now! Right damned now!"

Pearline's voice was ribboned through with love and sadness and a kind of pity almost. "Oh, Billy, sweet Billy. It doesn't work like that. It won't ever work like that."

"What are you talking about? Why not?"

"Billy, Fergus Blackthorne is the richest man in Salt Springs, and Nicholas is a little colored

boy without a last name who works dumping spit-
toons in Honey's, and nobody's going to take up
his side against a man like Fergus!"

"But that's not right!"

"Not right, but so. Not right, but so."

Billy's boot heels on the new fresh floor.
Step and a drag. Then I heard Billy start to cry.
"Damnit, damnit, damnit," he said all the while,
and then Pearline's tip-tap footsteps crossed to
him, and I knew they were holding each other
close and his tears were in her hair. Pearline
must have starchy petticoats on; I could hear
them crinkle and crack. Then, there was their
footsteps moving in the direction of the front of
the schoolhouse, slow and in unison. I lifted my
head as best I could, and pretty soon they come
into my seeing as they moved across the slope
that ran down to the trail. They had their arms
around each other's waists. There was no talking.
If they'da turned around and ever looked back
to the schoolhouse, they woulda seen me pinned
up there on the roof. They never turned back,
though. They just kept moving away, both of
them with their heads down. They still weren't
talking when they went around the bend and
were out of sight.

There wasn't any doubt in my mind that I
couldn't stay perched up there on the roof like
I was, just like there wasn't any doubt that staying
up there was exactly what I wanted to do, because all the trouble in the world was down there

on the ground. I laid my head back and just
stared up at the clouds, the way a boy might do,
seeing faces and puffy-cheeked monsters gliding
by up there. I remember doing that way back,
when a whisker was just something on a cat. It
was a good time, simple as a piece of pie, easy as
the clouds I was looking at. But life has its way
of tugging at your shoulder and bringing you
around to look at the real things, the things that
are hardly ever easy or soft, and right now, the
way life picked to do that was the pretty basic
need I was feeling to get down on the ground
and take me a pee. I reached over and grabbed
on to the hammer, started to unhook me from
the roof. I took my time.

The bunkhouse was empty by the time I got
back to the Starett place. Hef probably had the
boys out rounding up the last and the lowest, getting ready for the drive after the Fourth. No sign
of Billy or the Dutchman or anybody else. Cookie
told me Billy had come by, but said he didn't
stay more than a minute, said Billy had asked
about me.

"He say why?"

"Bobcat, he said."

"Talk sense."

"I am. That's what he said. He'd been out to
the schoolhouse, he said. Saw a bobcat out there.
That's why he wanted to see you."

"What the hell am I supposed to do about
a bobcat?"

"Oh, I don't think he was looking for you to do anything. He was looking for you because he wanted to borrow your gun."

"Lord, God."

"I told him a pistol wasn't the thing, that I'd go on up to Mr. Starett's and see if he'd give out the loan of one of his rifles, that a rifle was the thing for that kind of game, but Billy just shook his head at that. Needed a revolver, he said. Then he just stomped on off."

I leaned back against the cookhouse door. My head was winding around itself in a bad way. I closed my eyes, trying to stop the spinning.

"You all right, Wilbur?"

Straightened up, stiffened up, nodded. "Tell Hef I'm taking a horse off the remuda. I got to get into town."

"Where's Geezer?"

I didn't answer Cookie, just took off out the door. Geezer wasn't important anymore. Hardly anything was.

It was sliding to dark by the time I got into Salt Springs. I looked over in the direction of the corral when I rode past the livery stable. Geezer was standing there at the rail, looking at me on another horse for the first time in our time together. Poor Geezer. That musta been a hard puzzle. People or beasts, it all comes down to a hard puzzle.

Rooney's was crowded when I walked in. I stood there for a time, looking around slow for Billy, but there wasn't any sign of him. That pushed me off step. He couldn't go to Honey's, and every shop was buttoned tight.

"Help you, Wilbur?" It was Rooney, belly out, hair slick and shiny.

"Looking for Billy Piper."

"You found him sort of, but not really."

"I'll just wait here till you sober up."

He grinned, gold tooth center stage in his mouth. "He came in about three hours ago and started drinking like he was looking to put me out of business. After he passed out at the bar, I walked him into the back room, let him sleep it off."

"He got a gun?"

"Billy don't wear a gun, Wilbur. You ought to know that."

"That wasn't what I asked, Rooney. What I asked was whether or not he had a gun."

Rooney's face went under a cloud. He didn't like being talked to the way I was talking. "He was wearing a duster, Wilbur. I couldn't say what was under it. I got work to do." Rooney turned away.

I moved for the back of the place. Hadn't taken more than three steps before I felt Rooney's hand on my shoulder.

"Where the fuck you think you're goin', cowboy?"

I didn't turn back, kept looking at that door in

the farthest back wall of the place. "I'm going to check up on my pal, that's all."

"Well, he don't want to be checked up on, Wilbur. He said that over and over. Let him sleep, he said. He had rough thinking to do. He said it over and over. Rough thinking to do. Don't get all tight-jawed on me, Wilbur. That's not like you."

Now I did come around to talk this to his eyes. "And it ain't like you to screw down on a customer who's only looking to check up on a pal."

"He wants to think a thing out, Wilbur."

"You're an adamant man, Rooney."

"I am."

"Why?"

"Wilbur Moss, we are talking about bothering a man who don't want to be bothered, a man who is going to teach my Deidre about learning out of books, learning things I do not know, things her mother never had a chance to know. And mister, I am telling you that if Billy Piper can do that, then Billy Piper is going to be left alone to do some thinking, for as long as he wants, and I won't see it done any other way." His lower lip was all shoved out, like a five-year-old protecting a puppy. His eyes sparkled with growing wet. He stood solid in front of me. There were people starting to watch us. I'd lost.

"Deputy," Rooney said. "I've got other things to deal with. I think we're done talking. Is that what you think, too?"

It was the word "deputy" that did it for me. Like it or not, and it was not, it was still my job to protect innocent citizens from getting hurt, and that realizing inside closed off all the switches that might let me get off the track. "Keep him here for at least ten minutes, Mr. Rooney. Can you at least do that?"

"Can and will."

I nodded, touched off the brim of my hat, and moved outside to the walk in front of Rooney's. Looked the street one way and then the other. Nothing to be seen except Forrester's hound out on his rat patrol. My steps on the boardwalk seemed loud, too loud, but there wasn't a thing to be done about that. I was doing what needed to be done, and loud walking didn't apply as being important. I swung over across the street and went past the livery stable, past the barn, and then to the corral.

Geezer was there and moved to the fence where I was standing. I reached out and took his head between my hands and rested my forehead against that soft white blaze of his. He didn't move and neither did I. He snorfled once or twice, but didn't back away at all. I don't think I knew up until right then that I loved Geezer a lot. I patted his neck, stroked him a time or two, then moved off to where I had to go.

I stopped when I got to the middle of the street, looking off in the direction of Honey's, more afraid than not that I might see Pearline in her hooded robe come out the door with Nicholas by her side, but all there was in the street was me. I started walking on, and thought for a second I heard Nicholas playing on that sweet potato, but it was my mind twisting the night a little. The sky was clear as good well water, so there was no problem seeing the white carpet of the night sky. Just like looking at the clouds earlier, looking at the stars took me back a way; wheat stalks snapping in a crisp breeze while me and my buddy stared up and wondered things we didn't know how to put into words. I almost stumbled when I got to the boardwalk on the other side of Main. You got to stand still when you look at the stars.

I walked as soft as I could, hitched up my belt, checked what needed to be checked. There was a little spill of orange light coming out of his front window. I knocked three times. Heard footsteps coming to the door and stopping just on the other side. "Who the hell is it?"

"Deputy Wilbur Moss, sir."

The door got pulled open hard and he stood there. A sour wave of bourbon sweat came out into the night. "What the hell is this all about, Deputy?"

So I showed him.

Wasn't more than two minutes later before I was standing in front of another door. I hadn't seen another soul while I was walking, except for Forrester's hound, that trotted by me with something black and wriggling between its jaws. I knocked on the door, then took a couple of steps back. I put both hands around behind me.

"Who is it, please?"

"It's Deputy Wilbur Moss, ma'am."

Mrs. Willard Ganeel unlatched the door and opened it wide. "Wilbur. Come on in."

"No, ma'am. I'll just wait out here. Like a word with Willard, if I could." He'd heard me from inside, and there was a chair scrape and he came into view. His suspenders were down and there was a napkin tucked in at his shirt collar. He motioned Mrs. Ganeel back into the room and she went right away, a woman used to being motioned away.

"Wilbur."

I brought out my left hand from behind my back, extended it out to him.

He looked down, took half a step back. "What's that?"

"Marshal, that's the gun I used just now to kill Fergus Blackthorne." I was holding the gun by the barrel. There was still a little heat to the steel.

VIII

There was just too much that Marshal Willard Ganeel just could not puzzle out. The notion that anyone had got himself murdered in Salt Springs was upside down enough, but you add to that the factor that the murdered man was linchpin to everything that was going on, and that the killer was Marshal Ganeel's deputy, and he was as hamstrung as a man gets to be. He had me manacled to the rail of his porch while he went off to Rooney's and tracked down Mr. Starett and swore in Omar as his newest second in command. There was fractious debate as to where to put me, being as Salt Springs never had seen need to build an official jail, being used to dumping drunks into the little cage added on to the back of Ganeel's General Store.

That's how I ended up in Blackthorne's barn, same place where we took Billy after he got hard mashed by Black Iodine. They added some boards to the sides of one of the stalls, and screwed on a flange and a lock to the door. I had a stool and a blanket and a slop bucket and a view of Omar sitting ten feet away from the stall gate with a lever-action balanced across his knees.

Every once in a while, I looked down at my right hand, the one that lifted the gun and put the barrel right in the center of Blackthorne's forehead, the one with the finger that tenderly squeezed the trigger till there was that hard flat "pop." I clearly closed my eyes when the shot happened, and the kick snapped my wrist up, because when I finally opened them, all I saw was a puffy cloud of gray smoke where Fergus Blackthorne's face had been just a second before. I remember I leaned forward and looked down on his face where he was laying. It surprised me that the hole was so little, with a delicate fringe of pink flesh around the dark part. Fergus's eyes were opened wide and had a set of disbelief about them. It seemed a shade odd to me that the last fireworks Fergus was destined to see didn't come on Fourth of July, but from the barrel of the gun I brought to his doorstep on my own version of Independence Day. But sometimes, things work like that.

I heard a wood creak, and looked over to the door to see Mr. Starett standing there. He started toward the boarded up stall that was my cell.

"Not too close, Mr. Starett," said Omar.

"Willard was real clear about not letting anyone get too close."

Starett didn't let on he heard a word, never taking his eyes off me, but he did pull up fifteen feet or so away. His jaws were working hard, but there was no chew there. He was just clenching down on what he had to say. "You treacherous piece of horse flop," he said.

"Yes, sir."

"You know what you did?"

"Yes, sir."

"You mind telling me why you did it? Why you blew the brains out of an innocent man who never did harm to another living soul?"

He was a nice man, Starett. There was no point in getting disputatious. "Mr. Starett, I had a reason. Might not add up to a proper cause for you, but I had me a reason."

"You know how much you hurt this town?"

"I don't see that."

"This is just what the railroad and oil people were afraid of. This could turn them around." His face looked like the back of a ladybug, all red with dark speckles.

"Mr. Starett, as long as there's oil, they'll keep coming. We could be a tribe of three naked cannibals, and they'd keep right on coming."

Omar grunted a kind of laugh. Mr. Starett looked back at him sharp. It'd be some time before Omar grunted another laugh in Starett's hearing. Mr. Starett swung back around to me.

"We're getting word to Cody and Judge Dewey. You know Judge Dewey?"

"Never had the pleasure."

Starett's neck was close to overflowing his collar. "I didn't figure you'd be social friends with a circuit judge, Wilbur Moss. What I meant is whether or not you've heard of Judge Dewey."

I nodded.

"And his reputation. You've heard of his reputation?"

I gave another nod.

"He'll be the one coming to Salt Springs to hear your case. I wouldn't take much comfort from that fact if I were you. As a matter of fact, if I were you, I'd be damned straight afraid."

"Mr. Starett, I don't know how I could be any more afraid than I am right now, so you can leave off all the effort to make me even more afraid, because I think I reached my limit quite a time back."

Mr. Starett wasn't pleased about me trying to save him all that internal commotion. He came loaded for bear and I kept acting rabbit and he didn't like any of that, not one damned little slice of it. He turned and walked out of the Blackthorne barn like a man who had to pee at a fancy dinner who didn't want to miss dessert.

"Wilbur, I need some advice." It was Omar talking.

"I'm an odd choice for advice, Omar."

"You're not actually. You've had experience

with being a lawman. And I've got a lawman question to ask of you." His face was pruned up. He was breathing deep.

"Ask away."

"Marshal Ganeel gave me stone-hard orders about not leaving you alone, Wilbur. He was very forthright about that."

"I haven't heard a question yet, Omar."

"I need to use the outhouse, Wilbur. But that would mean leaving you in here by yourself, which Marshal Ganeel was very forthright about not allowing." Omar stood up and took a few steps closer to my stall. "So, I want your word that if I leave here, you won't try to escape."

"I'd need an ax to get out of here, Omar."

"I still want your word."

"You'd take my word? I put a bullet through a man's brain about six hours ago, Omar."

"I know that."

"And you'd take my word?"

"I would."

"Take the word of a murderer, you would?"

"There's nothing to say that a murderer can't be an honest man. And that's what I think you are. Yes, you killed Fergus and there's laws about that, but you went straight on over to Marshal Ganeel's and told on yourself and that's what an honest man would do." Omar hooked his thumbs in his belt and pulled his pants out from his gut. "I'd appreciate hearing your reply,

Wilbur. Time's running out for my lower bowels, I'm afraid."

"You got my word, Omar. I won't budge. I'll be here when you get back." Omar smiled at once and turned away, heading out the back door in a wide-legged waddle. When he slammed the door shut, I stood there for a time looking around the little space they gave me. There was a certain restfulness about where I was and what I was looking at. I'd always prided myself about being a man with a good hold on the reins, a man who could turn any way that appealed to him and go where he wanted when he wanted. That was all gone now. Instead of being a man at the wheel of a ship with control of the rudder, I was just balanced on a little board now, bounced back and forth by a spinning sea of currents. Scary in some ways, but easy in others, because I had no choice to make about anything; all I had to do was stay balanced and see where I ended up. I lay back on the blanket and closed my eyes. Way off, I could hear some little girls singing a jump rope song. Forrester's hound started barking about something. A wagon went by on the street outside, supply wagon sounded like, wheel noise too heavy and low to be a two-up rig. Fergus Blackthorne was rotting old meat in the back room somewhere, and I was facing trial for murder, and the business of Salt Springs wasn't missing a tick. Then, I heard the front door hinge squeak its song, and knew someone was coming in. A few seconds later, I heard a step, then a foot drag, step and a foot drag, step and a foot drag. Billy Piper come to see his pardner.

"Wilbur, you awake?"

I sat up. "Looks like, yeah." I looked past Billy to the front door. Pearline was standing just inside. "Hey, Pearline."

"Hey, Wilbur." Her voice had a tremble to it.

"Rooney told me you were looking for me last night," said Billy.

"I was."

"Rooney told me you asked whether or not I was carrying a gun."

"Rooney's doing a lot of telling, isn't he?"

"Did you ask him whether or not I was carrying a gun? Did you?"

"I don't see as it matters, Billy. I'm not in this damned little box because I asked too many questions."

"You killed Fergus?"

"I did."

"Why?"

"He needed killing, Billy. We both know that. He needed killing."

"You don't kill a man for no reason."

"There was a reason."

Billy put both hands on one of the new boards they nailed over the stall gate. "And do we both have the same reason in mind, Wilbur?" His eyes never left me. I looked away, but I knew his eyes never left me.

I was losing my balance on that little bouncing board. I wasn't sure my voice would be there or not. I just nodded my head. I heard Pearline give out a soft moan.

"I need you to say it, Wilbur. I need to be sure. Was it about Nicholas?"

Was and it wasn't, but I couldn't tell him that. I couldn't tell him what got done to Nicholas was black and hard, but that the other thing was heading off Billy before he took and threw away all the years he had still coming to him. I couldn't say that to him. That'd put an anvil on his back for the rest of his days. Couldn't say it to him. Couldn't. "Once a man does what Fergus done, he's just wasting air and taking up space. I moved to address that error."

"How'd you find out?"

I was a heifer being herded down the chute. No way left, no way right, no way to turn back. "You and Pearline were out at the schoolhouse yesterday afternoon. I was up on the roof. I heard."

Billy looked back over his shoulder at Pearline. Their eyes talked to each other, asking, answering.

"Didn't neither one of you say anything that needs regretting, Billy. Nothin' like that got said."

He didn't look comforted. Neither did Pearline, but it didn't come to anything because Omar came back in through the door and started yelling, waving the lever-action around, telling Billy to back away from the stall, telling Pearline to stand still and not say a word, that he was the law here and things were going to be done the way he said they had to be done. The news about the new doctor coming in had taken some sorta toll on poor Omar.

Billy lifted both hands high, edging his way back toward Pearline at the front door. "Omar, let loose of the reins a little. We're leaving right now. Stop pointing that thing over here. We're no bother to you."

"You just get on out of here! No one's supposed to be in here without my permission!"

"You weren't here when we came in!"

"Goddamnit, don't go throwing that education blabber to me! You shoulda got my permission!"

"You weren't—" Billy stopped when Pearline's hand rested on his arm. He swung around to me. "Honey's trying to get in touch with a law counselor in Cody. He's helped her with some legal knots she's gotten into before."

"Billy, what the hell's the man going to do? I did what I did. He can't change the facts. Even a lawyer can't change the facts!"

Pearline was tugging on his arm. They were close to being out the door. "Wilbur, you're going to go to trial. Everyone who goes to trial has to have someone to talk for him! That's the way they do it!"

Omar was still at full cock. "Out-out-out! And if you come back, bang loud on the door and let me know who it is!"

The door was starting to swing shut when

Pearline called out, "Wilbur! Is there anything I can bring you?!"

"Cigars!"

"OUT!"

The door slammed shut. Omar trotted over to it and slammed the bolt. Omar walked back to his chair. He was puffing. He let out a groan when he sat back down. "You shoulda called out when they come in."

"Figured you were busy."

"Still shoulda called out."

"I'll remember for next time."

"Appreciate it."

"How're your lower bowels?"

"Better. Thanks for asking."

I couldn't get a tighter grip on how come everything was slowing down for me, but there was no questioning that it was doing that very thing. It struck me that a man in a plight like mine, charged with murder and looking to do a rope dance if it went bad, ought to be nervous and twitchy, but it was the other side of the river with me. I was sleeping like a midwinter bear and eating like it was a one-price-eat-till-you-bust. I had me Omar during the day, and Rooney would send over one of the long-necked enforcers for the nighttime, though they mostly tended to nod off after it got too late and they got comfortable. Didn't change my life one way or the other; I was sleeping, too.

Pearline was good as her word about the

cigars, and she was quick enough to show up with one for Omar, too. He wasn't sure about letting me have one, said he thought I might start a fire and escape. I pointed out that a man locked in a place who starts a fire in that same place is buffalo dim at best. He saw the point and enjoyed his cigar.

Fourth of July was hearing the bugle and drummer leading the people to the corral and speeches from Starett and Omar, not to mention a puff-belly railroad man who said the president of the railroad was all thrilled about getting rails into Salt Springs. There was a musical selection from Vera Monroe, and a recitation from John Everett Malone. I couldn't see the fireworks, but I could imagine them, going on the crowd chiming in after each explosion, and what I imagined was almost for sure better than what was being seen outside the barn, where they was keeping me. Lord knows I was in prison, but Lord knows I was free.

The fifth of July was notable only because of the tattoo of muffled drums that went past late in the day, close onto sundown. I knew it was the funeral procession for Fergus Blackthorne. When the rig wheels of the casket wagon went by, there was a whole lot of footsteps, but that was no surprise. People turn out in a prime herd when a rich man dies. Might be even more so when the dying happens with a little bit of help. Blackthorne would be buried in the place right next to his wife, who we planted nearly a year before. Hell wouldn't hold no fear for Mr. Fergus Blackthorne.

The hinges squeaked again, and Omar and me looked up from the game of checkers to see Billy standing there with a short man in a fat suit. It just seemed the suit was the fat part, not the man, because everything about the suit was so tight. Vest was shiny black, and you could hear the buttons ache with each mincing little step. The shirt was starched sun-bone-bleached white, and you could have bounced dice off the front. The pants turned his bottom half into something like a wool sausage, and his shoes had an inky glow. Billy walked him over, and Omar allowed him some space.

"Wilbur," said Billy, "like you to meet Eve Pacquette. Eve's from Cody."

"Eve? Your name is Eve?"

He was used to this. Didn't drop a stitch. "Y-V-E-S," he said. "It is a French name. But yes, it is pronounced 'Eve.'"

"Mr. Pacquette is the lawyer I told you about. He's worked with Honey. She feels real strong on him."

"Shit on a duck, I got a lawyer named Eve."

He pushed out his lips, shook his head. "Mr. Moss, we'll need to talk before either one of us knows whether or not I'll end up representing you." He swung around his whole body to look at Omar. "You're the jailer?"

"First assistant deputy."

"Well, First Assistant Deputy, I need to talk to Mr. Moss."

"Go ahead."

"In private. A lawyer and his client meet in private."

"I just heard you tell Wilbur you didn't know for sure if you two was going to hook up at all."

Pacquette looked to Billy for help, then walked off to the other side of the stable. He took care where he stepped.

"Omar, I think you better go get Marshal Ganeel," I said. "We need a decision here and I'm not sure you've got enough cartridges in your belt to get us that decision."

Omar looked down to his belt. "I'm not wearing a—"

"Go get Willard," I said. "It'll go easier all the way around."

That appealed to Omar. "You promise not to escape?"

"We promise," said Billy. Pacquette looked over at the three of us, trying to understand, then deciding it wasn't worth his time. He watched Omar scurry out the door, then came over to us. "Is there a place we can meet in private?"

"There's the back room at Rooney's."

"And Rooney's is . . . "

"Saloon halfway back on the other side of the street."

Pacquette's expression took on some verve. "I

remember passing it. I think I'll go over there and wait for you. It's been a long day and I could use a little bracer myself. A touch of the restorative." He gave a little bow and moved after Omar's route. When he closed the door, it was a quiet thing.

"We're going to get you out of this," said Billy.

"How? I did it."

"Pacquette will find a way. He'll use the law. The law's got all sorts of twists and switchbacks. There's ways lawyers know that regular people never hear about."

We were quiet for a time. Billy and me had gone through a lot in this old barn. Seems like we weren't through yet. "Can I ask you a question?"

"Sure."

"When I came looking for you last night at Rooney's, were you carrying a weapon?"

"Would it make a difference to know?"

"It would. That's why I'm asking, Billy."

He hunkered down. His index finger drew some curlicues in the dirt. He looked back up at me. "I had a gun. I knew the Dutchman kept one in his trunk. I took it."

"You think you might have gone and used it on Fergus once you got sobered up?"

"No earthly way of knowing, Wilbur. That's what I had in mind when I came in to town. But if I had to get drunk to go through with it, there's no telling what I might have done. But taking Fergus down was in my mind."

I smiled inside. "Then what I did was the right thing to do," I said.

"You did him so I wouldn't? Is that the way?"

"Billy, count it out. I got what, five years, ten years more? You got fifty, maybe sixty. The ticket's a lot cheaper for me than it would have been for you."

He looked at me for a long time. His jaw worked on itself.

The door banged open, and Willard Ganeel was standing there with Omar at his shoulder. There was something dangling from his right hand, something shiny that made a chiming metal sound when he started in our direction. It was only when he told me to hold out my hands that I saw they were cuffs and shackles he was holding. I stuck both hands out over the stall rail, and Willard made quick work of fastening them around my wrists. He still had a pair left over. I don't know why he'd brought two pair, for God's sake. He nodded to Omar, who set to work unlocking the front gate. Billy stepped back when Omar opened the gate wide and I walked on out.

"Far enough," Willard said. He nodded to Omar, who dropped to his knees and started to work the second set.

"Oh, Jesus, Willard."

"There's rules," he said.

It took Omar a couple of tries to get them around my boots, but when it was done, he looked up smiling, like a kid finally tying his own shoes.

"A horse gets hobbled, Willard. Not a man. I don't eat out of a trough or shit in the street. This ain't right."

"There's rules," he said again. "I checked with Rooney. The back room's available. Let's go."

I started forward, and almost went on my nose, the length of chain was so short. Billy grabbed hold of my elbow and kept me upright. I started again, and could only take little tippy steps. I felt myself start to hunch over, pulling in somehow, my head going down. It was god-awful, the worst feeling I ever had in all my days, humiliating and hard. Billy still held hard to my arm when we got out onto the street. Omar and Willard were right behind us, and Willard had drawn his sidearm. People on the boardwalk all stopped and looked while I made my way to the other side of the street, moving like a gut-shot deer just before it goes down.

"Almost there," Billy kept saying. "Almost there."

A couple of little girls out with their maw hid behind her skirt and peeked out around her, looking at me. One of them pointed. They both giggled. Their maw hushed at them, but they all three kept looking. When we got to the board-walk, the chain was too short to let me take a full step up, so I had to half hop up to the boardwalk level, getting my feet under me with a boost from Billy at my elbow.

"Almost there. Almost there."

"Willard? How about we go in the back way?"

"Front door's quicker."

"Dammit, Willard, I don't want to be paraded in through the bar."

"Front door's quicker."

There weren't many people in Rooney's when I was hobbled in, but there was a few, and any was many to my present way of thinking. I knew most of who was in the place, but there was no hellos or nods. They looked at me the way you'd look at a blood spitter in the Miners' Hospital, like I'd crossed some bridge that put me out there with the animals and boot heels covered with horse dump. I just kept my eyes straight down on the floor. It was wet, just now mopped.

"Almost there. Almost there."

Pacquette peeled himself away from the bar and followed after us. The glass in his hand was brim high with an amber liquid that I didn't think was apple cider. We got to the back room door, and Billy reached out and turned the knob, pushing the door open ahead of me. I hitch-hopped to the nearest cane-back.

"Get the leg irons off, Omar."

"I don't take orders from you, schoolteacher. You're not my—"

"Get the goddamned leg irons off now!"

Omar looked at Willard, and got a nod that let him get back down on his knees and start working on the leg irons.

"We'll be right outside the door," Willard said to Billy.

"Then get there, Willard. I'm anxious for you to be on the other side of the door."

I'd never seen Billy take on that much granite before. He knew about determination from the ground up, but it was always quiet before. There wasn't any quiet in the way he was looking at Willard Ganeel. The marshal and his first assistant deputy moved out of the room and the door got itself closed.

Mr. Pacquette put his glass on the table, though within easy reach, and proceeded to take the floor.

"Let me tell you about this case as I understand it from a purely legal standpoint. Obviously, you both feel you know more about this case than I do, and that's perfectly understandable, but often when someone comes in with a fresh perspective, he can point things out that those who have been more closely involved might have overlooked in the heat of the moment." He took a sip of the drink, patted his lips dry with the back of his hand, pursed his lips, licked them, and went on. "As I understand it, there was substantial bad blood between you and the late Mr. Fergus Blackthorne. Would that be an accurate assessment thus far?"

I cleared my throat and shrugged. "He was a hard man to like, I guess."

"And he was very active in your selection as deputy?"

Billy shook his head, stumped. "What in the hell you trying to build here?"

"Well, I can't build anything if you keep interrupting, can I?" Billy allowed as how that was probably true, which gave Pacquette the time to take another sip. Lip pat. Lip pursed. Lip licked, he went on. "And as the man largely responsible for your becoming deputy, wouldn't it also make sense that he would be responsible for your getting paid for your services?"

"I get paid by Mr. Starett."

"For being a hand on his ranch, yes. All well and good. But did you ever receive payment for your contributions as deputy of Salt Springs, Wyoming, Mr. Moss? It's a yes-or-no question."

"Well, I don't recall ever getting paid specific for the deputy part."

Pacquette clapped his hands once. "And there you are. A poor old cowhand willing to put his very life on the line for this town and its citizens, and the government of that very city refuses to pay his due!"

"Mr. Pacquette—"

"And that sad sorry cowhand decides to confront the man shorting him! Needing an understandable boost to his courage, he stopped in to the local saloon to get himself a drink. One leads to two and two leads to three and so forth and so on."

"Damnit, Mr. Pacquette, that's not why I stopped at Rooney's!"

"Old-timer, do you want me to help you or not?" His next sip emptied the glass.

"Well, sure I—"

"Then damnit man, keep your mouth as shut as your long-john trapdoor and we might have a chance! Lonely old cowboy gets righteously angry and decides to do something about it. The old cowboy—"

"Stop calling me old!"

"—and he gets himself skunk drunk and goes on over to the stingy lying sonofabitch who's cheating the old guy out of his rightfully owed money!"

"That's not why Wilbur stopped at Rooney's," Billy said. "And he's damn well not going to lie about it."

Pacquette's look was lizard calm. "He's willing to put a bullet through an unarmed man's skull, but he's got qualms about telling a little white lie that might save his life?" He looked back and forth between me and Billy. I nodded. Billy nodded. "All right, you tell me. Why did Deputy Wilbur Moss stop by Rooney's before sauntering over dead sober to fire off the fatal round?"

Billy and me looked on each other. Pacquette saw the look and stepped in quick. "Anything you tell me will be held in secret. It's attorney-client."

"How do we know we can trust on that?"

"Young man," Pacquette said, "I am a lawyer." He spoke the last word like he was ending a prayer.

I pointed a finger at Billy, as I didn't want any part in telling what Fergus Blackthorne had been up to. I didn't have the words, and even talking close about it seemed to me like wading into turpentine and sheep dip.

Billy didn't welcome me stepping off to the one side on this, but it didn't look like he was surprised much either. He kept Pearline out of it as much as he could, and never brought in what Pearline did for a living. He said it was all reported by a person about a girl from Honey's being sent out to service Fergus, with Nicholas brought along for that music, then the dove never getting touched and Fergus taking Nicholas into a separate room, with Nicholas telling what happened after the second night at the Blackthorne house. That's what had gone on, said Billy, and that's what got Wilbur Moss fired up enough to go on over there and do what got done.

Pacquette looked from Billy to me and then back to Billy again. He had the kind of smile you see at a kid's Christmas pageant. "Gentlemen," he said, "there is no judge and no jury that's going to do spit to the memory of the richest man in town on the basis of what he's rumored to have done to a little nigger boy." He held out his pudgy hands. "I get the sense that isn't what you were hoping to hear, but I'm just giving you the benefit of my years before the bench. They won't harm the memory of a rich white man over a nigger boy."

The only sound in the room for a long time was Billy's index finger tapping on the top of the table. He pursed his lips like he was going to give out a whistle, but all he did was breathe out long and slow. "Mr. Pacquette," he said finally, "it looks to me like your glass there is bone dry. Why don't you go back in to the bar and order another one. Tell Rooney to charge to me. He knows me; it'll be fine." Pacquette beamed and snatched up his glass. When he opened the door and left the room, we got a quick glimpse of Willard and Omar standing on the other side. They peeked in like me and Billy were naked ladies.

Billy closed the door hard and leaned against it for a time before he swung around to look at me. "I thought he was a good idea, Wilbur. Looks like I was wide of the mark. You think so, too?"

"Billy, I'd rather try to give a close shave to a slab of raw calf's liver than have to deal with that walking tub of oil slime."

"I'll talk to Honey again; maybe she knows somebody else."

"Why do we have to talk to anybody? What's the point?"

"Wilbur, I said it before. The law's a complicated thing. We need a man who knows how it works and what needs to be said. You need somebody to talk for you."

I always hate it when a thing seems so clear to me and all clouded up to other folks. The older I got, the more that was seeming to happen. "Billy, what's he going to do? I did the thing. You know that, I know that. Everybody in town knows that. I wasn't drunk. I wasn't crazy on anything. I knew what I was going over there to do, so I went on over there and I did it. I'm guilty as guilty gets to be."

"He needed killing. That's what you said to me."

"Why? Why did he need killing?"

"Because, damnit! A man can't do things like that without someone holding him accountable!"

I kept my voice low. Billy was the last person in the world I wanted to argue with along about now. "Billy, that's my point. I did a thing and they're going to hold me accountable. I knew that was in the wind when I walked up to Fergus's door."

Some wind went out of him. "You want to die, Wilbur?"

"Nobody wants to die." I thought that over, then: "Well, hardly anybody, and I'm not one of them."

"And that's why you need someone to talk for you." He grabbed a chair and pulled it over. "Yeah, you're guilty and, yeah, that's how they're going to find you. But that won't be the end of it."

"What will be?"

"They can decide to fit you for a hemp tie or to send you away for the rest of your days."

"Not much of a choice."

"It's the only one you got, pard."

I lowered my head and lifted my hand, looking to cover my face. When the hands came up, the chains clinked together. What a sour dismal sound of surrender. I put my hands back in my lap. "Death doesn't set me on edge, Billy. Death is darkness, and I'm not a man who's afraid of the dark. Dying, on the other hand, grabs me hard and low. The thought of dropping through a trap-door with a canvas bag over my head, of being jerked up suddenly and having my neck broke, if I'm lucky, or just hanging there like the bottom string on a shade, twitching and dancing and being choked out, that's a play I don't want to see."

Billy's look was soft. I needed that look. "They'll want to send you to prison for a long time, Wilbur. It'll end up being a life sentence, even if they just put it out as a number of years."

"I know that."

"So that's what you want to happen?"

"It's better than dyin', is all. It's about the only good thing you can say about prison, I guess. It's better than dyin'." I straightened myself up in the chair. "But I'm a tough old bird, Billy. There'll be days when I can see the sky and feel the wind and hear the thunder bouncing off the sides of the mountains. I heard once they know the old buzzards don't look to go over the wall, that they let them work in places doing little work. Note keeping and library things and working in places like that. If I got that, there'd be other old buzzards I could talk with and lie to. It wouldn't be as easy and good as the bunkhouse, but it might be tolerable. Especially when there isn't any other choice. I might end up being the best prisoner they ever had."

"You old sonofabitch."

"Thank you."

"And that's why we have to find someone else to talk for you in court. We need to make certain you get those blue skies from time to time."

"What's wrong with you?"

"All sorts of things. What are you talking about?"

"How about you being the one talking up for me in court?"

His head started moving back and forth right away "Wilbur, I'm not a lawyer."

"We just talked with a lawyer, Billy. He's smooth as mercury in butter and not worth much more than that. He's a lawyer and I don't want a lawyer. I want you to talk for me."

"You need somebody who knows the law, somebody—"

He stopped when I lifted my right hand. I took care not to let the chains talk. I waggled my index finger back and forth. "I'm at a place where just making a choice, any choice at all, is going to be more and more a seldom occurrence. There's going to be people telling me where to go and where to sit and what to eat and what to wear, what I can and can't say and do and maybe even feel. My fault, nobody else's, but that's what got dealt to me. So be it. So, what I'm trying to do here, Billy, is make one of the last choices I'm ever going to get to make in my natural life. And my choice is you to talk for me at the trial. Are you going to tell me I won't get the chance to make that one final choice? You going to tell me I ain't got that right, that I just got to go in the direction I get pointed by whoever's got the badge to do the telling?"

The door banged open and Willard stood there. Omar was behind him, hand wrapped around the butt of his Colt. "What the hell's going on in here?" Willard said.

"Talking. We're talking."

"You're lying! That porky lawyer of yours is at the bar drinking corn and sweating stink."

"So?"

"So this little goddamned parlay was for Wilbur to talk legal with his lawyer! I'm looking around the damned room, and guess what—I don't see any lawyer in here with Wilbur!"

And Billy Piper said, "Look harder."

IX

Every afternoon, I get to go out into the corral behind the barn and walk around for half an hour to get some air and sun. If it was Marshal Ganeel in control, I had to wear the leg irons. If it was Omar guarding me, he'd let me go out with just the hand manacles, which helped make the air sweeter.

Geezer was out there, too, and it seemed like I was forgiven for putting him in there after Heflin's cigar butt had done its damage, because him and me would walk around the corral time after time and I'd talk low and he'd snorfle when the mood took him. I'm not all that brain-fried, so I really do know that Geezer didn't understand a thing I was saying, but that wasn't important or mattering. What was mattering in a tilted way was that there was another heartbeat next to mine, because being in a place where you're the only heartbeat is real close to not being at all.

I got more and more easy with talking out loud to an animal that couldn't understand a word. There was never anyone around, so I didn't concern myself much with someone hearing me and putting me in the same bin with the addled and aggrieved. I was certain about my brain footing, so at first I was scattered some when I started hearing a voice talking to me. It was a Thursday, pretty much middle of the day, when a woman's voice said:

"Wilbur, I got some beer and deviled eggs here."

That's what an angel would say, so I don't know how I reacted when I looked all around and ended up seeing Pearline perched there on the top rail. Pearline is pretty as sun on new wheat, so I expect I reacted in a way she was used to seeing and probably came to like.

"Hey, Pearline." I started walking over to her, as it was an Omar day for me.

"You hear me about the beer and deviled eggs?"

"I'm walking to you, ain't I?" I motioned her to lower the tin with the beer, so I could block off Omar from seeing it if he stuck his head out of the barn. Pearline got it right away. I don't know what chilly gold must taste like, but I'm betting it's close to what that first sip out of a Rooney's take-along tin tasted like when it hit the back of my throat. She saw that and she smiled.

"Pearline, this is a kind thing."

"Billy's idea."

"You're the messenger; you get the ribbon."

"He found some books on law in Miz Starett's batch and he's reading up as fast as he can."

"Why?"

"Wilbur, he's defending you. That's what he told me."

I chewed on one of the deviled eggs for a minute. Geezer was edging in toward us, seeing an edible on the nearby. "I'm guilty, Pearline. I don't see a defense. I did it. I told people I did it. Defending doesn't change what's so. If it does, it's amending, not defending."

"He doesn't want you to die, Wilbur. You know Billy; he's out to make the world perfect."

"I hope not. I hope not for your sake."

"What do I have to do with it?"

"You and Billy want to be together. You and Billy want to be together in some other place doing something other than what you're doing now. But if Billy's out to make the world perfect, he's going to come in the door every night of his life mad and frustrated and filled with sour things inside. A man lives like that, pretty soon the sour things win out."

"How about 'better'? Suppose he only wants to make the world 'better' instead of perfect?"

"Still a hard thing."

"Good things are, I think."

I switched my look to her, and a part of me marveled at women and the kind of strength they got inside. I don't know how her life didn't twist her smile or make her eyes go dark, but the mark it left on her was inside and didn't touch anything vital. "Billy Piper's a lucky man," I said.

"I know." She held out the take-along tin and I took a final sip. "Aren't you afraid, Wilbur? Aren't you afraid at all?"

"Not of anything on the top side of the grass."

"What does that mean?"

Geezer pushed on my shoulder. I looked at Pearline, and her smile handed me permission to hand him a deviled egg. It went down like a gravy gulp. "What it means is that I put my gun barrel right up into the middle of Fergus Blackthorne's forehead and pulled the trigger, and all there was left was a smaller hole than I thought would be there and no more Fergus Blackthorne on the face of this earth. And while I've never been a believer as some would have said it, while I wasn't that before and haven't confirmed into one now, I can't stop myself from wondering what it might be like on the other side if the thumpers are right and there's an old white-haired man wearing a heaven dress waiting for me and he asks my name at the gates and he listens, and then I can't stop myself from wondering what he's likely to say to me, knowing what I done to give Fergus Blackthorne a quick boost over the final fence."

"That's easy, Wilbur. I know what he's going to say."

"Which would be?"

"That old white-haired man's going to say: 'Welcome home, cowboy.'"

I didn't have anything to say that words could help out with, so I just took another sip of beer out of the Rooney's take-along tin, and Pearline just was a pretty bird perched on the top rail of the corral.

"Schoolhouse is going to be finished by the end of the week," she said.

"You got to be wrong about that, Pearline. Billy couldn't do all that by himself in that little time."

"Well, he's not doing it by himself, not anymore." Her look sneaked quick at me, then danced off. She wanted to see how I was taking it. "Mr. Starett took most of Blackthorne's men and put them out there working on getting it all done. And it's not just the schoolhouse anymore."

"If it's not just the schoolhouse, what the dickens is it?"

"Well, it's going to be used for other things when school's not in session."

"Things like what?"

"Things like you being tried for killing Fergus Blackthorne."

I was going to go on trial for my very life in the very building me and Billy Piper put up with our own two hands. Shit on a duck.

She saw my eyes and hurried on, trying to put butter on the burn. "It's all part of how Mr. Starett wants Salt Springs to look big and settled down for the new people coming in. We need to have a place where it's like church, a place where important things happen. That's why he moved so quick to make sure the building was up and solid and pretty as a picture. It's all to impress the new people."

"I wouldn't want to go on trial in a place that wasn't pretty as a picture, Pearline. It'd be an awful thing to contemplate." I heard the back door of the barn open, and knew Omar was standing in the door in total glower. I raised my arms high overhead to show I wasn't about to smuggle a Gatling gun back into the barn, then turned slow to face him.

"Time, Wilbur," he called out.

"Coming in, Boss." I looked back at Pearline and nodded my best, then resumed walking back to Omar. The barrel of the rifle was pointed to the ground, but it was cocked full.

"Billy's going to come by tonight," she said. "Lawyer things. Legal things."

"I expect I'll be here." I moved in past Omar. His nose wrinkled up when I passed him, smelling the beer.

"Next time that woman shows up here bringing you a beer, you tell her to turn right on around and get out of here."

"Suppose I told her I'd just drink half the tin and bring the other half on in here for you."

His mouth worked like he had a bad tooth way

in back. "Yeah, that'd be a way of doing it, too, come to think of it."

Billy thought I was sleeping when he showed up that night, but that wasn't so. I had started spending time behind closed eyes, but hearing everything and knowing what was going on, sort of floating through time, avoiding everything I could, knowing that there were parts of me that were getting more brittle and frail every day and that crawling into a kind of hole and pulling the dark in after me was a way of being able to handle the harsh brightness when it came time that I couldn't avoid it any longer. So, I heard him when he came in through the door, exchanged heys with Omar, and moved on to the stall cell. I sat up.

"I like seeing Pearline better," I said. "She brings beer."

"Smells better, too, probably."

"I wasn't going to bring it up, but it's something you might want to work on."

Billy smiled. He turned a bucket over and sat down on the other side of the door. He had himself a bunch of papers in his hand. "I need to let you know what's going to happen when we get in to that courtroom."

"Pearline tells me it's a building we both know pretty well."

"That's so." He looked down at the top sheet of

paper. "I'll take this slow. You need to listen hard. You got a question, you pop up and let me know."

"Go."

He took a breath, turned his head back and forth, though he wasn't wearing a buttoned up collar. "It'll be formal in there. They'll put the judge up on the front platform."

"Where you were going to put the teacher's desk."

"Just where."

"All right. He's up high in front. What next?"

"He'll ask you your name."

"He doesn't know my damned name?"

Billy waved a hand, letting me know I needed to step back and work on the listening part. My look let him know I understood. "He'll know your name, but he'll have to ask for the record. I told you it was formal. He just needs to get down on paper that they got the right man in front of him."

"All right."

"Then he'll ask you how you want to plead."

"And I say guilty."

"No. You say not guilty."

"Billy, you know and I know—"

He slapped his hand down hard on the stack of papers. "Wilbur, get out of my way and do what I'm telling you to do! I'm trying to save your life here! I don't know if I can keep you out of prison, but I might have a long shot chance at keeping you using up some air and not just helping the grass stay healthy! If you plead guilty, they'll send the jury home and it's up to the judge to say what's going to happen. If you say not guilty, that means I'll get to call a witness or two and maybe get them to thinking they need another look at what you did and why you did it, and that might mean they won't be building a platform with a trapdoor in it just meant for you!"

"You'll call a witness, you say."

"Maybe more than one."

"Who? And what would it be that they'd be a witness to?"

Billy turned and looked back at Omar by the door. "It's time for that privacy again, Omar."

"Sonofabitching pain," Omar said. He got up and moved to the front barn door. "I'll be right outside here," he said.

"We know. We'll try not to take long." Billy watched the door, and waited till Omar was out of the barn and the outside latch got slammed shut before he moved around to look at me once more. "The witness would be Nicholas."

"And you'd ask him questions." Billy nodded. "You'd ask him questions about what?"

"About what Fergus Blackthorne made him do."

"Billy, Lord God. Talk about that stuff out loud in front of all the people likely to be there? That's harsh on Nicholas, Billy. That's clawin' off a scab."

"Wilbur, we're talking about your life here."

"You said there might be more than one witness."

"I might call Pearline. She didn't see what happened, that was all behind closed doors, but she could still talk about other stuff." He saw the dark come over my face. "What? What's the matter?"

"Billy, I'm not sure if you got an idea about how much I don't like sounding like a lawyer, any lawyer, and that lawyer Pacquette in a special way, but I don't see any way out of it. What he said before, cobbed as it was, still had some rock at the bottom. You think you can talk against a murdered rich man with the word of a pleasure woman and a little nigger boy like Nicholas?" I didn't like talking about Pearline and Nicholas like that, and I could see Billy didn't like it much either.

"Well, why don't you give me the list of people you think I ought to talk to, Wilbur? I'll just wait right here while you're coming up with that list of yours." If Billy coulda taken the look he had now to the poker table after a draw, there woulda been folded hands going down all around.

"All right, I ain't got no list," I said. "And maybe I don't have any chance either."

"It's not a big one, pardner. It's a slice of potato you could read through."

The door opened quiet and Omar was standing there with two men. Their clothes were wrinkled and dusty and their clothes said they came in to Salt Springs in a rig, not on horseback. City clothes. Pale soft city faces. Omar cleared his throat. Billy spun around to see who came in. He got up at once and started off to them, never looking back to me once, which told me whoever these two were, they were there to spit in the soup.

Billy moved to Omar and the new two at the door, and they started talking, but low, too low for me to hear a word. There were handshakes all around and Omar backed off like a mutt in the parlor with the queen's cats. Billy said a thing, and the two new ones looked over at me. They were looking at me, but I wasn't there; I was just that thing they were looking at. A few more words and a few more nods and Billy started walking them over in my direction. They both took off their hats. The old one had frizzy gray hair; the younger one, shorter with little quick chicken peck steps, had his hair shiny and combed perfect. Billy's hand gestured to them both when they reached my stall. "Judge Andrew Dewey, Mr. Hugh Walsh, like you to meet Wilbur Moss."

"Mr. Moss," the old one said. Young one just bobbed a nod.

"Hello," was the best I could do.

Billy had himself all pulled up, church-usher proper. "Judge Dewey's going to be presiding at the trial, Wilbur."

"If you say so."

"And I'm the state's attorney, Mr. Moss. I'm the lawyer for the other side." You'd have to boil his eyeballs before that look of his would ever nudge up to cool. "Do you have any idea why Judge Dewey and I stopped by to see you, Mr. Moss?"

I looked at Billy, shook my head.

"They're here to see whether or not there ought to be a trial, Wilbur."

The two both saw the look in my eyes, baffled, lost. The old one took a try. His voice sounded like he wanted to help. "The law doesn't like killing, Mr. Moss. The law doesn't even like it when it's the state itself that might be doing the killing, especially if the person to be killed isn't up to realizing the facts surrounding the decision that's putting his life at risk in the courtroom."

It was in view now; I could see it. I held up a hand, palm out. "I'm not too dumb to know what's going on and I've never been crazy a day in my life, especially not on the night I knocked on Fergus Blackthorne's door. I did what I did and that's why there's a trial and I got no excuse, no excuses."

Billy came in quick. "Wilbur, you do have a story to tell. That's why we're going to call in some witnesses, remember?"

The young short one threw his fang in. "And, Mr. Moss, you do realize that Mr. Piper here isn't really an attorney, don't you?"

"I do."

"Do you realize that I'm regarded as a very good attorney at law, and that I'll do every legal thing in my power to convict you?"

"That's your job. I expect you're good at your job. Your coat looks expensive as perfumed gold." I smiled. He didn't smile back.

Judge Dewey cleared his throat, though it didn't need it. "Sounds to me like we're done here, Hugh. Nice to have met you, Mr. Moss. We'll be seeing you in a couple of days." He could have been talking about a horse auction. Him and the young one started backing away. The judge talked on the move. "I don't run a merciless court, Mr. Moss, so if there's some request that crosses your mind, something you might need or something that might assist Mr. Piper in mounting your defense, let us know. I'm not going to promise we'll grant everything you might come up with, but I will give it a fair hearing. I'm not a man who rules brutally from the bench." He did what he did to pass for a smile; then the two of them was at the door. Omar pulled it open for them,

"Hey!" I yelled out.

They looked at each other, then to me. "Yes, Mr. Moss?"

"I do think I got me one request."

It was something I'd wanted to have done ever since my voice changed and I started knowing what being a man was about, though I never got to a hundred percent about most of it, when I look back. But it was a thing I seen in every pissant town and village and city and populated pimple I was ever in since my squeaky days. I've stood at the window and watched in just about every one of those towns, but it involved paying out money and money was meant for food and drinks and sweatin' the sheets to good purpose, and I could never see my way clear to rolling the silver out for something that frivolous. But when the judge spoke out like he did and I realized I might get it for free, I thought it was worth the effort to at least holler out. To my surprise, and Billy's, too, the judge laughed out loud and said as he didn't see the harm.

So I was going to get me my first barbershop shave.

Quentin Tillman didn't call his place a barbershop, because he had been to San Francisco and knew about the word "tonsorial." It was a little place behind the bathhouse and the sign was in small letters: TILLMAN'S TONSORIAL. The letters were pint-sized, I suppose, because Tillman's main business, The Floral Funeral Parlor, was just down the street and Quentin didn't want to confuse the public. There was understandable speculation as to whether Quentin got his practice on the dead so he could make the living look better, or if, in fact, it was totally the other way around. Didn't matter spit to me. If my shave and a haircut helped some rotting hulk look more presentable to those who loved him, then so be it. If it was the other way around and some corpse was helping me look and smell my best, then I voted with Judge Dewey; what's the harm.

I toyed with the notion that it might also be that Quentin could trim me up today and then have me to work on later on in the week, when I might have crossed over, but that's the kind of thinking that gets you down and dizzy, so I shoved it aside.

It was Sheriff/Marshal Willard Ganeel in the saddle today, so I was outfitted with hand manacles and leg irons again. I had to hop down off the boardwalk down to the street, and getting to the other side was slow goin', me moving like a gut-shot pheasant. I don't know what it was about those leg irons, but they brought my head down; they beat me. Even going to Tillman's Tonsorial, which is exactly where I wanted to be, those leg irons made me more of a prisoner than I ever wanted to be.

Today was the day Billy was going to talk with Nicholas, after Pearline smoothed the way talking to the boy last night, and maybe after I had tasted heaven with my haircut and shave, Billy would walk in with some news that sparkled in the dark.

Give Quentin Tillman his due; the man treated me like I was a visiting fat belly from Moneytown when I was hopped in by Willard and Omar. He talked about seeing me stop in front of his windows sometime and how much he wanted to cut that head of hair because, according to Quentin Tillman, the head of hair I had was just about the best head of hair ever got Wyoming wind blown through it. He was saying all this in that bird-chirpy way of his, and while I knew it all had more bullshit than the Goodnight-Loving Trail ever dreamed about, it still made me feel better about things. Quentin kept up his chirping even while Willard was making sure Omar was getting both my hands cuffed to the arms of the chair.

"Willard, you really got to do me like this?"

"Do."

"Why?"

"Quentin's going to be using a straight razor at some point."

"So what?"

"You might try to grab it, kill yourself."

"Willard, if I was looking to kill myself, I'd just bust out running when we were crossing the street. 'Cause you'd use that shitter to blow me in two. You know you would."

"I would. Never said I wouldn't. But I wouldn't take no joy from doing it. Just because it was my duty, that's all. Wouldn't take no joy at all."

Quentin had me swing around, facing the mirror. He was ducking side to side, left to right, fluffing up my hair like a woman does to a pillow. Felt good. "Well, Willard, in that way, you and me are alike," I said.

"What way?"

"If I was to cut my throat, I wouldn't take no joy in it at all either."

Quentin put his hands on each side of my head and tilted it to one side, then pressed hard on it like he was setting a cornerstone. I took what he meant and tried to stay stock still. A sheet got wrapped around me and the snipping started. It was a pleasant sort of sound, steady and pleasing. The little feathers of hair tickled when they touched me on the back of my neck, and I couldn't think back on a time when I was tickled past the age of six or so. It didn't take Quentin long, as he was good at his job and I wasn't a grizzly sort on top. He combed my hair with a soft brush and stood back, letting me look in the mirror.

"Mr. Tillman," I said, "that looks just—"

He put the tip of his finger to my mouth. "We are not done yet," he said.

Then the chair got tilted back and I was looking up at the ceiling for just a second, before I was looking at nothing at all after he wrapped a steaming-hot towel all around my face. It was hotter than Hell and I tried to pull it away, but when you're cuffed to the arms of the barber chair, there's problems about doing that. Tillman put a hand in the middle of my chest, and the heat got bearable and he could feel me relax and go back onto the cushion. The towel had some kind of scent on it that made taking in slow deep breaths a good pastime. Quentin started stropping the razor in a slow even way, strop one way, then strop back the way he came. Slow and slow, like one of those tippy metal fingers piano teachers use to keep the counting regular when they've got a kid there on the bench. Way off somewhere, I heard laughing, young laughing, so I didn't have to peel away the towel to know there were kids with noses flat against the window glass looking at the scary man chained down to the barber's chair. I didn't have to look and I didn't have to care because it was just like when I was drifting away when I was up on top of the schoolhouse just a few days ago. More and more, I was finding ways to go back on into myself and curl up tight in a little cave back in my brain and let it all go by at its own speed, not of any concern to me at all, not while I was curled up tight in that dark cave protecting me.

Quentin stopped the sound of the razor going back and forth on the strop and proceeded to peel away the towel off my face. I kept my eyes shut, smiling because I'd seen enough barber shaves, standing at the window just like those kids on the boardwalk, to know what was coming next, and it was better than I hoped when that warm lather got brushed out gently on my face, something so soft and clean it just seemed that this must be what they make clouds out of.

While he was finishing the brushing, Quentin said: "You don't seem at all nervous."

"About gettin' shaved?"

"About going to trial."

"That's up to Billy. I'm just riding drag."

"Hope it goes well."

"Makes two of us."

"You sign papers for your belongings?" I didn't say anything, so Quentin went on. "That horse of yours seems sturdy enough, and you got your saddle and all the gear. If it doesn't come out right, you want to make certain all that stuff doesn't go to the wrong people."

"Quentin, sounds like you're trying to shave me twice here. Once for whiskers, once for stuff. Let's just concentrate on the whiskers for now. We clear?"

"We're clear," he said. "Hold still now."

Quentin was an artist with that straight blade of his, could have carved butterfly wings into anvils if he was of a mind. He'd go over every little patch twice, taking off those little pin-feather whiskers a man finds with his tongue about halfway through the day and worries at till well on the other side of midnight. If he buried as well as he gave shaves, I might not choose to attend when the Resurrection Day stomped on in.

I heard the door open and then Omar murmured, "Hey," so I was safe in thinking it must be Billy who had come in. Quentin made a shushing noise, and a couple of steps told me Billy was on one of the waiting chairs. Quentin put away the razor and brought on a new towel, not as hot at the first one, but scented still. He cranked up the back of the chair, then unwrapped me a second time and I was seeing Wilbur Moss like never before. Not young or handsome, not that ever, but just more pulled tight and together. I made Billy's eyes in the reflection in the mirror. The expression was set straight and level. "How do I look?"

"Like a man ready to arm wrassle the Devil's own."

"That's an off-step way of putting it."

"Might be, but I think that's what you better get ready to do, Wilbur." Billy unfolded out of the chair and moved up behind us. He put one hand on each of my shoulders. He looked to my reflection, me to his. "I went to Honey's to talk with Nicholas. Went to his room. It was empty. All his clothes were gone. He's run off. We don't have us a witness anymore, Wilbur."

Quentin stepped forward. He had a bottle in his hand. The slosh in the bottle was the color of a horse fly's stomach. "You want some cooling aromatic to finish up with?" I heard Quentin, but it was off some as I was taken up with just staring at Billy Piper's face in the oval mirror. Quentin took my not saying anything as being the same as saying yes, so he splashed a puddle onto his palms, then smacked it all over my cheeks.

Stung like a sonofabitch.

Later on in the day, me and Billy and Pearline were in the back room at Rooney's. I knew that things were sour and bad because Willard Ganeel had let me leave Tillman's Tonsorial without the leg irons. Wasn't as much diversion for the kids on the sidewalk, but I was grateful. It was too early for serious business at Rooney's, so the room on the other side of the door was stony still. The room we were in wasn't any different.

Billy had asked Pearline to go to Nicholas last night and talk to him about what was going on, what a trial meant, and what he was going to be expected to do. Now he asked her to tell everything that got said when she did that, and she agreed to tell, but a couple of minutes had gone past since she said so, a couple of minutes of her staring at the floor, swallowing back tears, gnawing hard on her lower lip, then squeezing her eyes shut.

I couldn't stay still that long. I nudged Billy. "Anybody got a notion which way Nicholas went when he took off?"

"There was footprints behind, leading off in the direction of One Legged Indian Crick."

"So he's not headed to the mountains."

"Wish he was."

"How come?"

Billy looked like a man at the end of a long drive in bad times. He rubbed his face. "The railroad's come about five miles the other side of One Legged Indian Crick. If he gets there and gets himself on to one of those supply trains heading back for a reload, there's pretty much no way of telling where he might get to after that. I don't know as we'd ever be able to track him down."

"I went up to his room about seven o'clock," Pearline said out of nowhere.

Billy and me looked over at her. Her eyes were shut and she'd pulled her knees up to her chest and had both her arms wrapped tight around them.

There were little rocking motions back and forth while she sat in the chair. Billy waved me to be quiet. We both waited.

"He was lying on the ticking mattress looking up at the ceiling, with his hands behind his head. I remember thinking it looked like the way a grown man might lie, but not a mostly boy. I pulled up the three-legged stool and sat down. He hadn't taken a shred of notice of me. 'How are you, Nicholas?' I said.

"'Fine. I'm all right.'

"'I know you heard about Fergus Blackthorne getting killed and Wilbur Moss being in trouble on account of it.' He nodded after a bit, still looking up at the ceiling. 'I don't know about you, Nicholas, but I got scared when I heard there was a murder right here in town. Did you?'

"'Seen fights before. Seen blood before.'

"'Well, yes, there are fights, and I guess a gun gets used by some of the Rooney rumpots, but this is different, I think. You and I know the man who got killed and we know the man who did the killing.'

"'Good.'

"'Good that we know the man who did the killing?'

"'No. Good that it was Fergus Blackthorne

that got kilt. I hope he comes back to life, so somebody gets to kill him again.'"

Pearline hadn't stopped rocking back and forth, hadn't opened her eyes. There were tiny wet diamonds glistening at the corner of those eyes. "I never saw a child's eyes like that. Even where Nicholas has been living, even with what he sees and hears, he was still a little boy, still had mischief and knew how to laugh and tease and play the way a boy will. But that was gone when I was looking at him last night. It was gone, burned out of him, the way you burn skin off the flank of a horse or a steer."

Billy's voice was a soft stroke. "And after he said that, what did you say, Pearline?"

She dabbed at her nose, breathed in through her mouth. "Well, I said, 'There's a lot of people who feel like you do, Nicholas.'

"'Then why's Mr. Moss in trouble?'

"'Because that's the way the law works. Sometimes it's hard to understand, but that's the way the law works.'

"'Not making much sense to me, Miss Pearline.'

"'That's why we're lucky, Nicholas.' He looked at me then for the first time since I came into the room. 'We have a chance to help Wilbur. We have chance to let people know why Wilbur did what he did to Fergus.'

"'How?'

"'By testifying.'

"'Don't know what that means.'

"I tried to imagine I was building a house out of little blocks, one on top of the other, slow as can be, making sure it all got balanced. 'They have a trial, Nicholas. There'll be a judge come in all the way from Cody. A very serious, very important man. And Billy Piper will be there. It's all going to be where we go sometimes to see Billy, out at the new schoolhouse. And all you'd have to do is to answer some questions as honestly as you can.'

"'Who asks?'

"'Billy Piper. And, I guess, another man.'

"'Who's the other man going to be? I know him?'

"'I don't think you will.'

"'What are the questions going to be about?'"

Pearline stopped. She was looking straight out at the wall on the other side of the room. What she was seeing wasn't the wall on the other side of the room. "I said, 'They'll be asking about you and Fergus Blackthorne.'

"Nicholas edged away from me. 'Why they have to know any of that?'

"'Because it's important to know what a bad man Fergus was, Nicholas. And the things he did to you were wrong. It's important that people know that Wilbur Moss found out about it and that's why he did what he did to Fergus.'

"'Why they got to know what he did?'

"'To show that Wilbur Moss is a good man who made a mistake, but made that mistake just to

make sure Fergus Blackthorne would never
do to any little boy, any child at all, what he did
to you.'

"His expression rolled over and over on itself,
all wreathed in doubt. 'I got to answer all the
questions they ask me?'

"'If you agree to testify, you'll have to swear on
the Bible, swear to God that you'll tell the truth,
the whole truth, and nothing but the truth.'
There was no way to not see how scared he was.
'It's the only way there is to save Wilbur.'

"He ticked off the names on his fingers. 'So,
there'll be you and Billy and Wilbur and the important judge and the other question man . . .
That's who'll be there.'"

Billy groaned and his head moved down. He
covered his face. "What'd you tell him?"

"I told him the truth. I said there'd be a lot of
people there. There'd be someone to take down
what got said. There'd be the marshal and his
deputy. There'd be the jury, twelve, isn't that
right? And there'd be a lot of people from town
coming. I told him the truth. Isn't that what I
ought to do?"

"Yes. Yes. You did what you ought to do. Yes."
Billy let out a long whistle. There was no tune to
it. "What did he say after you told him all that?"

"He said: 'How come that many people got to
be there?'

"'It's one of the rules, Nicholas,' I said. 'Trials

have to be out in the open. Trials have to be in public. One of the rules.'

"'And I got to say out loud in front of all those people what Mr. Blackthorne made me do?'

"'Yes.'

"'And there'll be somebody there to write it down, so it won't ever be lost or get forgot?'

"'Yes.'"

Billy stood up with a hand to the small of his back. He went to the door and put both hands on it, leaning hard, his back to me and Pearline. "What did he say when you told him that?"

"He asked if there would be any blacks there. I told him there weren't that many in Salt Springs, so probably not. And then he just rolled over facing the wall and waved me away. I told him you would be in the next morning to help him with some of the questions, but he just waved me away like he did before."

There was a rifle butt rapped on the door. "We need to get back across the street to the jail. Willard's wife is bringing dinner over at five prompt. She rares back if things go late and her food gets cold, don't forget."

"It'll be a minute, Omar," said Billy. He looked at Pearline. She was loving him all she could with her look back, but that was all she could do and it wasn't enough. Billy swung over to me. "Pal, we got some thinking to do tonight."

"What about?"

"You know there aren't any wild cards in this

deck, don't you? You know it's not going to be that you'll walk free away from this."

"I know that. I'm just hoping you'll find a way to let me have a few years of walking, period. If it's behind the walls of the Stony Lonesome, then so be it. I just don't want to hang, Billy. You know that."

He understood, that was clear. But I never seen him look so old and bent. "Wilbur, the reason I wanted you to plead not guilty was so that I'd have a chance to call witnesses for you, the main one being Nicholas. Now he's busted through the fence and is off to God knows where. We haven't got our witness anymore."

"And what is it you want us to think about?"

"Whether or not we should just plead guilty and hope I can get the jury to see fit to let you live out the rest of your natural span."

Pearline let out a soft frightened noise. She reached out a hand and put it on my knee. I looked down at that hand for a long time before I looked up towards Billy. "Let's just hope Marshal Ganeel's wife didn't cook up another trough of that hominy, johnnycake, and side meat again. I'm gettin' awful weary of that crap."

X

Next morning, I was seated cross-legged in the back of the Ganeel buckboard, hand-manacled and leg-ironed. Omar had the reins and he kept the team to a slow pace. Willard was squatted on the other side of the wagon bed, his lever-action across his knees. He was watching me the way frogs watch flies. The day was pretty as days get to be, and I was grateful for Omar's slow pace, as the wagon bed doesn't offer a softness to its passengers. The rough part of that job is that all the people on the boardwalk could slow up and stare as he drove me past, and even some kids could run after the wagon, just looking at me and laughing, yelling out a singsong rhyme that went: "Wilbur is a killer! Wilbur's gonna hang!" over and over and over again. I think that Omar looked back at that and touched up the team, giving them a little bit of their head. I was grateful to Omar for that.

He reined in some after we got on the road outside of Salt Springs and the kids gave up trailing after the buckboard. It was quiet again, and I wrapped that around me. I was getting good at that. Willard Ganeel didn't appear to have the same reaction. He was still giving me that frog look. We started up the rise, and that reminded me about where we were. My heart started to beat harder and quicker. That surprised me. I didn't think it mattered that much to me. I straightened up, looking past Omar's shoulder, trying to get my first good look at it.

It did matter to me; as soon as I saw it, I knew it did matter to me.

It sat on top of the little knoll and it was just like the little drawing Billy had first showed me when we were scratching out the foundation outline in the dirt. It was painted white and glowed in the new first light like a bridal veil on a beauty. The windows were in, the bell rope reached back from the pole to the schoolhouse, so it could be rung from inside. There were two outhouses in the back, GIRLS over one door, BOYS over the other. A big sign was out front by the path leading to the door and the letters on the sign spelled out SALT SPRINGS COMMUNITY CENTER AND SCHOOLHOUSE. I didn't carry any happiness inside about the reason for my being there, but I did tell myself that if things turned rank on account of this new plea, that if Billy couldn't persuade them to save the lumber for the gallows, that at least

Wilbur Moss would have left something behind, that there was a place that had been changed for the better because Wilbur Moss spent some time and effort there, and there's something to be said about that. I stopped feeling guilty about how my heart started to pound when I got my first look at the finished version of the sweet-smelling raw-wood puzzle me and Billy put together. It all fit. It was sturdy and fine, and a man ought to be allowed a touch of pride for having had a part in it being there.

Omar pulled the team up and hopped down to tie them off. Willard walked over to me and got down on one knee, pulling out a key from his vest that he used to unlock the leg irons. When they come free, he tossed them off under the seat.

"Marshal, I appreciate that."

"Don't go all Sunday school on me, Wilbur. It's just quicker getting you in and out, that's all."

I took that for what it was worth and managed to get to a standing position. Willard grabbed a handful of my shirt and started moving me to the back. There were some people filing in to the front of the schoolhouse, most of them looking back at me, then looking away as quick as they could. Heflin and the Dutchman were standing by the door and looking queasy. Mrs. Ganeel was there, too, and I thought I saw Mr. Starett duck in through the side door. Omar was waiting by the back of the wagon when Willard got me there, and Omar had his hand on the butt of his gun. Another pollywog turned frog with a badge.

The two of them walked me up the path and into the building. As soon as I stepped in, I thought of what Pearline told us Nicholas had asked her, if the trial was going to be like a show, because it was clear the answer was yes, it was. Maybe not even like a show; maybe it was a show all by itself on its own. They'd brought benches in and all the people were facing to the front and there was a tall dark desk put there. It wasn't what Billy would want for the school, so this had to be a special judge desk they got in just for the occasion. I'm not sure if I was supposed to be flattered or not.

Billy was sitting at a desk off to one side, and that's where Omar and Willard took me. He looked up when I got to the chair, and he was all embarrassed and I knew why in a second. "Never saw you wear one of those before," I said.

His hand went to the narrow string tie at his collar. "That's because I never have."

"You do the knot yourself?"

"Pearline gave me a hand."

I looked around the room. "I don't see her."

"Honey told the girls they shouldn't come."

"Why?"

"Thought it might not look good for you. Thought it might backfire."

That made me sad. A person shouldn't be

ashamed of just being in a room. A person's got a right. Billy read my face.

"They're doing it for you, Wilbur. They're doing it because they want it to come out right."

"Still don't like it. Maybe they could come tomorrow, huh?"

"Wilbur, if we stick to pleading you guilty, there won't be any trial tomorrow."

That brought a question to my face, and Billy read it like one of his books.

"If we plead you guilty, there won't be any witnesses for either side. Won't be any questioning back and forth. It'll just be me trying to convince the judge to send you to prison, nothin' more. And the other side's lawyer trying to talk him into the rope dance. Either way, it won't take anything like the whole day."

It took me a time to get all that into my head. "You mean that by the end of the day it all will be done. Whether I live, whether I die, I'll know it all by supper time."

"That's what I mean. Unless you want to change your mind."

There came a rumble of wood squeaks from the back of the room, and we turned around to the front door to see Judge Dewey come in through the door. I never saw a king, but the way he walked in was the way I figure a king must walk in to a place. He was wearing a city suit, but it was fine cut to my eye and I doubt it was made in Wyoming at all. He looked at the crowd as he moved up the aisle, smiling, moving his head up and down just a tad. Being as Dewey didn't come from Salt Springs, I knew he wasn't looking at people he recognized or knew. He was looking at people who he'd given the high privilege of looking at him. He didn't have to know a soul to know that.

Willard Ganeel's voice was louder than it had to be. "All rise," he said.

I snuck a look at Billy, and he nodded when he shoved his chair back and stood up, me doing likewise. The rest of the room was on their feet at the same time.

Dewey moved behind the big dark desk and sat down. He nodded to the crowd, and everybody was butt down right away. Some people coughed. Some people cleared their throat. Dewey looked off in the direction of Mr. Walsh, and Walsh looked back with a shared knowledge, the look power gives to power. Dewey looked back at the crowd. "Ladies and gentleman, my name's Dewey and I'm the judge here and I'll run the court as I see fit, and what fits is that there won't be any outbreaks of agreement or disagreement or dispute. Anyone who doesn't understand that will be given the opportunity to think it through in a jail cell." He moved his head back and forth then, like he was sweeping with his eyes. It got quiet enough to suit him. He looked over at Walsh, who beamed back. He had his hands on a sizable pile of books and papers stacked on his particular desk. "The State ready to proceed, Mr. Walsh?"

"We are, your honor."

"Mr. Piper, is your defense ready to take a shot at it?"

"Yes, sir."

"Then perhaps your client might like to enter a plea."

Billy put a hand under my elbow and pushed up. We both stood. Billy fiddled with his tie.

"Waiting, Mr. Piper."

"Your Honor, Mr. Moss pleads guilty."

A high-pitched voice perked out a "What?" For a time, I thought Pearline was there after all, but it was just young Walsh. He was on his feet with a sinkhole where his mouth used to be. His hands fluttered all around the big pile of books and papers on his little table. The hands were saying, "But all the work I've done. All the research and preparation." The people in the seats made a buzzing-bee noise.

Dewey used the gavel with some force. "Mr. Piper, that's not the impression we got yesterday when we talked with you and your client."

"Judge Dewey, me and Wilbur talked it over and we just came out at a different place." Billy was breathing hard. He cleared his throat. It was a real loud silence.

The judge glanced off to Marshal-Sheriff Willard Ganeel. "Marshal, I need to meet with counsel in chambers."

"Excuse?"

"Chambers. I need to meet with the lawyers in chambers."

Walsh popped up out of his chair. "Judge Dewey, begging your pardon, sir, but Mr. Piper isn't any kind of a proper lawyer."

Dewey gave Walsh the look you'd give a moving worm in your pie. "Thank you for the correction, Mr. Walsh. I won't forget it." You could almost feel the heat coming off the bench he sat on. His head tilted over toward Ganeel again. "Marshal, I still need to meet with counsel in chambers."

Ganeel looked like a duck hitting a patch of ice. "Judge, I'm not all that sure what you're talking about, but offhand, I don't think we got any chambers around here."

Dewey closed his eyes. "Marshal, there must be someplace where the lawyers and the defendant and I could meet in private."

And that's how it was that five minutes later, Judge Dewey and young Walsh and Billy and me were all standing in the boys' outhouse. It was a two-holer, so there was room, but it probably wasn't going to be a very lengthy type of meeting.

"Mr. Moss, it's important that I impress upon you the implications of you pleading guilty. I'm not trying to get you to change your plea, but merely to nail down that you know what you're doing."

"Yes, sir."

"You understand that by pleading guilty you give up any chance of the court finding you innocent. Ever. Any chance whatsoever."

"Yes, sir. I get that."

"Did Mr. Piper say anything to you that made you change your mind?"

"Well, yeah. You could say that."

"Mr. Piper? You want to explain what got said?"

Billy took in a deep breath. That was all right. The outhouse hadn't got used yet, so there was no stench. "Judge Dewey, we had a witness we were going to call, which we could do if we pleaded not guilty, but that witness has gone off no one knows where to, so we decided to go the other route. Seemed like the only way."

"And who is this witness? What would the testimony address?"

Walsh lifted a hand schoolboy-like. "Judge, if the witness and the testimony isn't going to come into court, I don't think it should come into this discussion. It might serve to prejudice the bench, sir."

Dewey's look at Walsh made certain their ride back to Cody was going to be long and uneasy. "'Prejudice the bench,' Mister Dewey? Is that what I just heard you say?"

"Just offering a thought, Your Honor." He skulked back like moose nuts on a snowbank.

Dewey massaged the bridge of his nose. He was still at it when he talked. "Is that it, Mr. Moss? Did the loss of this witness make you change your mind? Did you, do you, understand why this change makes sense?"

"Billy explained it and I went right along with his thinking."

Dewey opened his eyes. It was a look that would crucify anything coming back at him that he didn't think was up to muster. "You do understand that all you'll be allowed to do is offer some character witnesses and have Mr. Piper do a summation that counts on the mercy of the court to spare your life? And that I'm not a very softhearted man?"

That last item didn't need saying out loud. I just moved my head up and down.

"One more thing," Dewey said. "Mr. Piper?"

"Yes, sir."

"The court's time is limited and valuable. I understand that Mr. Moss knows a lot of people here in Salt Springs. How many character witnesses are you planning on calling? And let me inform you that ten would be too many."

"And two might not be enough."

Something happened to Dewey's face that was almost like a smile. "Suppose we compromise on five?"

"Six."

Billy was raising the ante when I was the only one who had anything to lose if he didn't have the cards. I must have voice-twitched a little and he looked over at me.

Dewey shook his head. "Five still sounds more appropriate."

"We could flip a coin," Billy said.

Walsh choked back a laugh.

"Mr. Piper," Dewey said, low and slow, "you're confusing a court of law with a gaming house. Your woeful lack of experience allows me to overlook your last suggestion. But the number five still seems most appropriate to me, and I need to warn you that the number four is taking on an increasing amount of allure with each passing second. And I strongly urge you not to overlook my remarks, as I am mercifully overlooking yours. Do you and I understand each other, young man?"

"You're talking in English, Judge, and I understand that language. Whether or not you and me will understand each other, it just seems too soon to say. Though I am starting to see the appeal of that number five you talked about."

"Then five character witnesses it is," Dewey said. "And I think our time in this little cubbyhole is done. Let's get back outside."

As soon as we stepped outside, we were there with Willard Ganeel and his leg irons. Dewey and Walsh kept on going. Me and Billy held up. "Willard," Billy said, "we're only about thirty seconds from being back inside the schoolhouse and you're just going to have to take those things off once we get there."

"Rules is rules," Willard said, and knelt down,

pulling up my pant leg. Chains got rattled. Locks got snapped. Billy stood by my shoulder.

"You nervous?" I said.

"Yeah."

"You think the character people will help?"

"Might. A little."

"Only a little."

"Just my guess, but yeah."

"What's the popinjay going to do?"

"Walsh?"

"Yeah."

"No idea, Wilbur. You're a first-time defendant; I'm a first-time lawyer. I know I get to call character witnesses and I know I get to make a talk on your side, a statement. And Walsh gets to make a talk against you."

"What's he going to say?"

Billy's shoulders hitched up. "I expect he'll talk about the facts of what happened on that night."

"You can send him home; I could make that talk myself."

Willard grunted when he got to his feet. He moved around behind me and took a fistful of shirt. "Time," he said.

We started our shuffle back into the schoolhouse. I couldn't stop myself from prideful feelings when I saw how fine it looked in the sun. "Billy," I said.

"Yeah."

"You know what you're going to say to the judge?"

"I got it pretty much marked off in my head, yeah."

"Is it any good? Will it do the trick?"

"Wilbur, I'd say we'll know about that by sundown."

"Well, then, okay."

Billy told me once about a book he read where a boy got to go to his own funeral. People had got the idea that he had got killed, so they had a service for him and the way it worked out, he got to watch the whole shebang from a secret hiding place, got to hear all the sadness that was left after people thought he was a goner. Listening to everything that got said about me when the character witness people got marched up to say what they had to say about me was a whole lot like what that make-believe boy had to be feeling.

First one into the witness chair was Heflin, and that stumped me to the boots. He talked about how him and me rubbed each other wrong a buncha times, but that I was a worker he could count on and a man, he said, whose word was rock solid and steady. He said he wished he had more of me on a drive. Billy asked him if he'd hire me on the next drive if the chance come up, and Heflin said he couldn't answer that easy, because with the railroad getting closer, he wasn't even sure there'd be another drive, that the railhead being so close, he wasn't sure there'd even be another drive out of Salt Springs, things were changing that much and that fast. That last part was called out of order, but I never heard anyone say what the order ought to be, so I wasn't sure about what that meant.

Rooney came up next, and he told about me never starting a fight in his place, even when it was clear that I was seriously squiffled. Rooney told them there was times when I stopped fights from happening, even when I was bourbon-noggered. I don't remember any of those times, so I must have been about as fish drunk as a cowboy gets to be. Rooney also talked about me being real loose with handing out pleases and thank-yous, and that pleased me deep down, because my maw worked hard on that with me. If I ever get to meet her in another place, I'll be sure to give her the thank-you for that that I never got to give her while she was here.

Shit on a duck, the Dutchman was next, though after he was all done, they could have left him off the list as far as I was concerned. He said good things, but he said them the way the Dutchman would. Said I wasn't a card cheater as far as he could tell. Said someone stole a rifle out of his kit, but he didn't put me on top of the list for doing it. Pretty much said I was the best of the lot, though the lot was a motley bunch at best, so it was being at the top of a list that you never even wanted to be on at all.

Honey was next, and she described her job as being a "social hostess" and there was some ripple of laughter there, but Dewey hammered that down right away. Honey was dressed like I never saw her before. The dress was soft and puffy and it was colored a rosy pink. She overdid the cologne splash a bit, but there are worse mistakes a woman can make. Honey spent ten minutes saying I had good manners and was a gentleman and that was a scant breed in Salt Springs. I hope what she said did some good, but there was a sizable amount of cologne in the air.

I'll treasure forever the look on Willard Ganeel's face when Billy stood up to call out the final character talker. "Call Omar," he said. Omar moved out from the chair that was behind the table where me and Billy were seated. Omar sat down at the talking chair and looked at Billy. He stretched out tall where he was, might as well have been waiting for First Communion. Billy asked him his name and got how long he's been in Salt Springs and all his time as handyman and medical man, coming out of his days in the Army. Then he asked how Omar came to know Wilbur Moss.

"It all depends on what you mean when you say when did I know Wilbur Moss. Salt Springs isn't a town like your city towns. You don't always get to know someone because you get introduced and shake hands, not like that here.

It might just be a face you see in Rooney's or Honey's or just out on the street and you ask someone who that is, and they might tell you that's Wilbur Moss, so that the next time you'd see Wilbur Moss in Rooney's or Honey's or out on the street, you might say, 'Hey, Wilbur' and Wilbur, he might answer back, 'Hey, Omar,' but all you know then is each other's names, but you wouldn't say you actually knew the man and what he was like. You just knew who he was."

"And how long ago would that be for you and Wilbur Moss?"

Omar stared up at the ceiling, pursed his lips together. "Best as I can think back, it's been ten or twelve years," he said. "But I wouldn't say I really come to know Wilbur till last year."

"And what made that happen?"

"When he was taking care of you in the Blackthorne barn after Black Iodine broke you up so bad."

"Mr. Piper," Judge Dewey said, "I'm getting the impression you know all about Black Iodine and what might have happened, but I don't and neither does Mr. Walsh. Maybe you could fill in the blanks for us."

Billy told it as best he could, the frog-flip by Black Iodine, the pulling in of Omar on account of his times in the Army Medical, and all the days after and what went on. The judge told him to get back to Omar.

"Why do you think you got to know Mr. Moss after I got banged up?"

"Well, I don't know as I got to know him, like you say, but I got to know the kinda man he was. Is maybe."

"How's that?"

Omar had a round face, and it looked odd when he wrinkled up his forehead and mouth like he was doing now. I was too far old and too far west to get tangled up in the war, but I'd seen enough who had to recognize the look that was coming onto Omar's face. It was the look of a man who was being made to go back to a hell he thought he left behind forever. He took in a long breath, then looked over at Judge Dewey.

"We're not going anywhere," Dewey said. "You take the time you need."

Omar let his head fall low and his shoulders lifted and dropped a few times. When his head came back up, he started to talk, but he kept his eyes closed tight. "In the war, I was a doctor's helper. Aide. Assistant. Call it how you want. And I saw things I never want anyone else to have to see. I seen boys sixteen bleed out, and seen wagonloads of arms and legs that got lopped off with bourbon to hide behind. I seen blind boys sickened by the smell of their own rot. And I know how damned hard it is on the ones standing by, how easy it is to turn away and go off looking for something that ain't wrinkled up with death and stench. But I never saw Wilbur Moss back off from taking care of Billy Piper, not one stitch. And there was times right after it happened when Billy was in a world of hurt, crying and thrashing and striking out for all he was worth. He would do anything he could to make the pain stop, and if hitting out at somebody helped some, then he was the one going to be doing the hitting out."

"I don't remember that," Billy said. He looked back at me.

"You wouldn't remember, not a bit of it. You were out of your head with the hurt. And when you'd get like that, Wilbur there'd wrap you up in a blanket, like you'd do with a hurt animal to keep it from hurting itself, and he'd hold you all wrapped up like that, still you trying to hit him, and he'd say 'All right, cowboy. It's gonna be all right. It'll pass, cowboy. Everything'll pass.' And you'd stop thrashing after a time, and Wilbur'd just stay there with the blanket holding on to you, rocking back and forth. 'We'll get through this, cowboy,' he'd say. 'We'll get through this just fine.'"

Billy looked back at me again. "I don't remember that at all."

"Well, that's how it was," Omar said. "And what I learned in the war is that a man who will stick and not get throwed away because of how hard that is, how much hurt just seein' hurt can bring with it, is a man who's got the right kind of steel to his spine." Omar slumped back against the chair. He'd done what he come to do, though I wondered how much opening that door inside had cost him. He got up slow and walked past Willard Ganeel, but neither one ever looked at the other one.

"Mr. Piper?"

"Your Honor."

"I count that as five character witnesses and I believe that was our arrangement."

"It was."

Dewey looked over at young Walsh. "Prosecution ready to make a statement in regard to the penalty ought to be handed out?"

Walsh got to his feet. "Your Honor, I'd like to request a day's delay."

"Why?"

"Well, the prosecution came in prepared to try this case on the presumption there would be a plea of not guilty. We assumed a final penalty statement might be days away."

"Mr. Walsh, I think the defense was presented with the same surprise you got handed. Mr. Piper, you ready with a penalty statement?"

"Am, Your Honor."

Dewey looked over the top of his glasses at Walsh. "Mr. Prosecutor, are you telling me a non-lawyer, a fact you enjoy reminding the court about, is more prepared with their case than you are with yours? Because I think that would purely stun a lot of people back at the courthouse in Cody."

There was a touch of plum shade creeping into Walsh's face. "Might Your Honor entertain an early luncheon recess?"

"Mr. Walsh, if all your arguments were as direct and succinct as the one you just made, your track record would be truly one for the legal pantheon."

Walsh beamed and said thank you, so I guess a pantheon was a good thing.

The gavel got hammered down once. "Lunch recess for an hour."

"All rise," Willard Ganeel called out, and everybody did, while the judge headed out to be the first in the buffet line Willard's wife and some of the church ladies had set out in front.

Billy and me stayed in our chairs. He wanted to study on what he was going to be saying. I didn't feel like going through a food line wearing manacles, looking like a staring target. I heard a noise off to one side, and saw Omar moving to the door. I spoke out his name. He turned around. "Thank you, Omar," I said.

He just shook his head and went out of the building. It had been a hard thing for him to do.

Billy was reading some pages with his handwriting on them. I didn't think he noticed me watching. "What'd you think of the character witnesses?" he said.

"Didn't know I was such a helluva perfect fella."

"You're not; they lied." He was smiling. He

looked away from the pages. "Thanks for the stuff I didn't know about."

"Omar lied, too."

We both smiled. He went back to his reading.

"He wrapped his hand around the butt of that revolver and pulled it clear of the holster. He took his thumb and brought back the hammer as far as it could go. That's what proved premeditation. He had that fully cocked weapon free of the holster and in his hand when he took a step onto the front porch of Fergus Blackthorne's home and knocked on the door and waited there for that unarmed man to come to the door, possibly expecting a visit from one of his many friends, possibly anticipating—"

"Counselor," Judge Dewey said. "We know what got done to Mr. Blackthorne. We even know who did it. The defendant told us who did it. *He* did it. What we're expecting you to deal with is why the State ought to put Mr. Moss to death."

I hadn't heard up until that minute anyone say it out loud, with its legal good clothes on. It made me cold.

Walsh poured himself a glass of water from the little pitcher on his desk. He took it down, dabbed off a tiny drop from his chin. "Your Honor, if I've gone off on a tangent here, I apologize to the court, but I felt the need to emphasize the especially cold-blooded and heartless nature of this murder. There was no woman being fought over, no gambling debt to be avenged. All there was was Fergus Blackthorne opening his door and finding a man there with a gun who put a bullet through the innocent man's brain. Can you imagine the horrified last thought of poor Mr. Blackthorne? Why? Why me? What could I have possibly done to warrant such a brutish execution? He died never knowing, and that's a harsh and horrible thing to have as your last conscious thought when you go, and that is why the State needs to extract the highest possible penalty from Mr. Wilbur Moss. He deserves, and should receive, not an ounce more mercy than he showed poor Fergus Blackthorne! He's earned his own death, and we have a responsibility to make sure he gets paid and paid in full!"

He made a lot of sense. If I'd have had a vote, Lord knows I might have voted on his say-so. Found myself thinking on where little Nicholas might be along about now. And once I started thinking on little Nicholas, I took back my imaginary vote from Mr. Walsh.

"Is that it, Mr. Walsh?"

"Yes, Your Honor. Thank you."

"How about you, Mr. Piper? You all ready to go?"

"I am, Your Honor. Thank you." Billy gathered up those sheets of paper with his handwriting on them. He squared them off nice, put them on the corner of the desk where he could see them easy.

While he was doing that, I swung around to look back into the back part of the room. At first I was surprised, being as the crowd had nearly doubled from what was there at the start of the day, even to a long line standing across the rear wall. Then it come to me that word had gone out that the plea was guilty and that there'd be some kind of ruling on how I was going to play out the rest of the game. Pearline was there now, standing next to the Arabian girl. Rooney was at the back wall, standing next to a ten-year-old girl; his daughter, I suppose. Heflin and the Dutchman and even Cookie were there next to Rooney's kid. Mr. Starett was there sitting in the middle. There was a space next to him, saving the place for Miz Starett, I expect. There was a bunch there waiting to see if I was going to get the worst or only the second worst. I didn't blame them. I was curious about it myself.

"Mr. Moss? Mind facing the bench, sir?"

I spun back to face Dewey. "Sorry. I'm new at this, Judge."

Dewey nodded over to Billy. Billy took in a deep breath and cleared his throat. Him and me had an eye lock; then I looked at the desk. I folded my hands, kept my eyes down. I listened harder than I ever listened to anything before, and maybe I even prayed, as I always felt like those two things were some way pulling the same rig.

There was a long quiet before Billy Piper began to talk.

XI

"You got the right to kill Wilbur Moss, and you won't hear anything out of me to say different. He's done what he's done and he's said that he's done it, and the law says that one of the things you can do is have Wilbur Moss taken out and killed. That's your right.

"But having a right and using that right isn't always the right thing that ought to get done. Even the law points down that road in a way; that's why they say you don't have to kill him, that there's other ways and things to consider doing. That's the law's way of telling us to tread lightly around here, the law's way of knowing as perfect as we might try to be, as perfect as some of us even think we are, that when it comes to taking a man's life, to telling him there's no more air on the face of the earth that's fit for him to breathe, we need to move slow, cat-tracking slow.

"Because there's a mystery about what

happened to Fergus Blackthorne that night. And when there's mysteries, we need to slow that pendulum in the clock and take all the time we need to get it sewed up with tight clean stitching.

"Here's one thing we all know to be so; nobody does anything without there being a reason. You scratch your nose because of an itch. You slam a hunk of beef onto a piece of bread and take a bite because you're hungry. A man looks at a pretty woman a certain way because he's got another kinda itch with another kinda hunger. But none of it gets done for no reason; there's always a reason.

"What earthly reason did Wilbur Moss have for doing what he did? You can turn it anyway you want, there's still nothing that turns up easy that answers the question. Wilbur Moss was a man who didn't start a fight unless he was rightfully fired up by what someone else spit out at him in the heat of drinking. And that's happened to every cowboy in Salt Springs from time to time.

"Mr. Walsh over there, thank you very much, said there wasn't any money debt between Fergus and Wilbur. There wasn't any card that got turned the wrong way between Fergus and Wilbur. And Fergus couldn't have had much of a land argument between him and Wilbur, being as Wilbur pretty much owns what he's wearing and what he's put on his horse's back. And, like Mr. Walsh said, thank you very much, there wasn't any women in the picture. Wilbur's past the age for that and Fergus, even though he was past the grieving time for his wife, still was never seen to go in through Honey's front doors. A man of some sizable willpower, it seems safe to say.

"Well, wait. Whoa now.

"Not right for me to point anybody off in the wrong direction, and I think I might have just done that very thing. Not that I meant to; I didn't, but still, it's something ought to be set right.

"Fergus Blackthorne never went into Honey's for a fact, but there's rumors that he had Honey's best brought over to him.

"Mr. Walsh, you can sit down. I'm not saying anything is a fact unless it's a fact, but there's a man dead and murdered and a man who might end up dead and executed, and there's mysteries we need to deal with. Might not solve a thing, but at least we can talk about them, because it'll help us understand why Mr. Moss did the terrible thing he did, and that could go a long way to helping Judge Dewey make up his mind about what ought to become of poor Wilbur. Might help Judge Dewey get some justice done. It's a powerful terrible weight we've placed on his shoulders, and we need to do everything we can to lighten that load. I know you think so, too, sir.

"Where was I?

"Oh, yeah.

"I was saying about Fergus not having any woman trouble that could have somehow set Wilbur off. Even when a woman got sent over by

Honey to visit Fergus, she was never over there alone, because there was always Nicholas, the little colored boy, going along there with her. It looks to me like Fergus wasn't only a gentleman, he was one who loved his music, because as most of you know, Nicholas always carried that sweet potato of his everywhere he went, so maybe Fergus asked little Nicholas to use his gifts to help the nighttime pass sweet. But we don't know, do we, so we can't talk about anything like it's a truthful fact. Nothing.

"All we know for sure is that Fergus is dead and Wilbur Moss admits pulling the trigger that did the deed.

"Oh. And that little Nicholas ran off from Salt Springs. No one knows where he is. And no one knows why he decided to leave town. No one alive knows, at any rate. No living person knows. No living person.

"I said before, the law's got the power. Still true. And it's got power in all directions, too. That means that not every case on trial gets ended up the same way, because the cases are different and the justice that gets handed out is different for the very same reason.

"There's some who'll think that if Wilbur gets a burlap hood placed over his head and a hemp rope tied around his neck and is standing on the trap when it gets sprung, that the world they live in is going to be a safer place. Doesn't matter to them whether the rope snaps his neck bone like a hickory branch, or whether he's left to choke and gag and gargle his own blood. Once he's dead, they'll say they put the monster in the ground and a stone on top of the tomb door.

"And they'll be half right. See, there won't be any monster in the ground. Only one there will be poor old Wilbur Moss, and that ain't no monster by anyone's stretch.

"You take Wilbur Moss off and kill him, you'll be taking away a touch of kindness in this world. Not from me, not from anyone sitting here in this schoolhouse. You'll be taking a touch of kindness away from one of the coldest places there is, a prison where a man's world gets shrunk down to the space of a double coffin, the very place where a kind word is more precious and rare than gold its ownself. You won't be any safer on account of Wilbur Moss being behind those walls. He won't ever get out and he knows that better than anybody. Wilbur's an old cuss and they put those old cusses to work in the infirmary or the library, if they even got one, or in any place behind the walls where an old man might keep his heart pumping. The punishment's going to go to the ones Wilbur could help, especially the young ones, the ones who think harder is better and life's a rassling wreck. Wilbur can tell those young men different, so that when they get out, they might not be thinking the way ahead amounts to finding the blood trail and following it hard. But if Wilbur's there to pass a word, they might not get to that fork, and if they turn the right way on account of something he said, then you might be living in a safer world. And your wife and kids and everyone you smile at on the street. You send Wilbur there for life, there's a chance your own very life might get better. You send him there to die, a little bit of you is going to die, too. And there's none of us gets enough life, so do any of us want to throw away even the least little bit?

"I said it's all about the mysteries, and that's still so. I don't know why the pastures get green in the spring and what makes the melt seem just the right size for the river and the stream. Don't know how a duck knows its momma the second it comes out of the shell. I been trying to read every book I can get my hands on, but there's no eternity long enough for me to read so many books that I'll know more than I don't know. That's a hard thing to settle with. We don't like not knowing. We don't like mysteries in our lives. We want the figures to add up just so in order for us to move on with things. And if we can't find the answer, we'll just make one up. The Indians got their spirit world that controls things, and gamblers carry rabbits' feet, and in other parts of the world they got Buddhas and holy cows, and it's all a way to get answers for things they don't have answers to.

"What we're dealing with here has mysteries about it, too. To some people, it's a mystery why a man like Wilbur Moss would go to Fergus Blackthorne's and put a bullet through his brain. There's others still wondering why that little Nicholas went running off into somewheres a few days before this very trial. Well, maybe we'll never know the answers. Maybe we'll just have to accept that there's some things we'll never be able to define the way you'd look a word up in a dictionary.

"But there are some things we know for sure.

"We know killing Wilbur Moss won't make the world one lick better, safer, or wiser. We know putting a man behind bars for the rest of his life, especially when the man is one who's lived a life that's all taken place in front of a horizon that's got no boundaries, that's a punishment that drills through to the marrow. And lastly, we know there's a chance here to do a right thing and doing things right is pretty much how anyone makes tomorrow a good fit.

"I think I'm done.

"Thank you."

The look on Judge Dewey's face was one I saw flicker around the edges all the while Billy was talking. It wasn't the one eye squeezed shut you see looking down a rifle barrel, but the eye squeezed shut and the rifle barrel was the only thing missing. He took off his little half-glasses and put them in a fancy cloth case that fit into his inside coat pocket. He kept looking at Billy all the time he was putting the little glasses away.

"Mr. Piper," he said, "if there had been a jury present, I would not have allowed you to proceed in the manner you did. Implication and innuendo and facts never entered into evidence have no place in a summation, even under the most lenient of standards. But being as I'm a jurist and not prone to make the legal missteps a layman might make as a result of your presentation, I decided to let you play the hand out. We're going to clear the courtroom now so I can do some reflecting about the appropriate penalty to be levied upon Mr. Moss." He looked over to Willard. "Marshal?"

"All rise!"

Everybody did, and we all stood there for a couple of ticks. Dewey looked over at Willard again. "Marshal, I'm staying. The spectators are leaving."

"Oh." Willard started waving people out the door, while Omar showed up with the handcuffs dangling in tow. He clamped them on me, and me and Billy started down the center aisle, last ones out. Pearline fell into step next to us, Omar close behind as we made our way out to the buckboard that brought us out. Mrs. Ganeel and her ladies were quick out of the chute, putting out coffee and fried bread and biscuits. It would have been awkward for Pearline to go through the line with the ladies on the other side of the table, so Billy went to get us something. I looked over at the schoolhouse. One boy was perched on the shoulders of another, peeking in through the window, like Dewey was going to signal them what he had decided. I felt a pressure on my hand. It was Pearline's hand lighting like a feather on mine.

"Wilbur," she said, "I should have said this at the very start, at the very next morning after Fergus died, but I want to tell you thank you, that I know you saved Billy's life."

"I just got there first, Pearline. Fergus needed killing. We all three know that."

She shook her head. "But he was going to do it, the same thing you did, and if you hadn't stepped in, Billy would be where you are now, and facing the very same thing. You saved his life."

"And he's trying to do the very same thing for me now, so we're all even up." I looked down at her hand on mine, and tried not to think the thought that was trying to swim up to the surface.

Billy came back with four cups of coffee. Omar came up and took his, then backed off to give some room. His grip never left the butt of his gun.

We blew on the coffee and sipped a little. If there was any coffee left over, we could grease the wagon axles. Every once in a while, we'd look over in the direction of the schoolhouse, and we'd see Dewey moving past the window, hands behind

him at the small of his back, a commander review-
ing a battalion of troops who weren't there.

"Waiting to hear, Wilbur," said Billy.

"Waiting to hear what?"

"How you think I did." He took a sip, looking
at me over the edge of the cup. He wanted to
know and it mattered to him.

"Straight up?"

"Straight up."

"Well, Billy," I said, "I don't know if we'll ever get
a chance to do something like this again, but if we
do, I'd appreciate you doing me a little favor."

"What favor is that?"

"If we come down this trail again, I don't never
want to hear you talking about me as 'poor old
Wilbur.'"

He grinned and coughed, spitting out some
bad coffee, and Pearline clapped her hands like
a little girl.

Then the rope from back inside the schoolhouse creaked and the bell started to ring. It had
an edge to the clang; it had a tooth-paining
flange to the tone. Didn't have to be pretty. Had
to do the job. The job was to let us know that
Judge Dewey was done with his pacing and he
was ready to tell us what was what.

Wood squeaks and clothes rustles and throat
coughs and foot scrapes behind us, like a strong
oak tree shedding its leaves all at once till it

stands etched naked, with a pillow of crackling orange around the hem. We stood there at our table till Judge Dewey looked over the room and nodded in a formal sort of way and everybody sat down, wood squeaks and foot scrapes again.

"Mr. Piper, would you and your client stand, please?"

We did that.

"Mr. Moss, you have anything you'd like to say to the court before sentence gets passed on you?" He said it without looking at us, scratching out something with a black pen on a little square of note paper.

"I got nothing to say because nothing I could say can change anything I done."

Dewey sat up straighter where he was. He put the square of paper down in front of him and smoothed it out. He lifted his head and looked at me and there was more hurt in the look than I was easy with. Billy reached out and put a hand on my shoulder.

"Wilbur Moss, you have pled to and been found guilty of murder in the death of one Fergus Blackthorne." He took a breath and looked from the little square of paper and eye-locked hard on me. He started to fold the paper in half.

Days past I'd told myself I'd made nothing but peace about everything that could happen, that I'd found a way to accept the cloudburst or deal with the flood, and I was disappointed when my gut told me what a liar I had been, even lying to me myself, because as Dewey took a breath, I could feel my heartbeat start to hammer like a trapped miner, thudding against my ribs like I'd swallowed a hawk eating a butterfly.

He folded the half into quarters. "It's the sentence of this court that you be—"

God. God. God.

He folded the quarter even smaller, then he pulled his coat away from his shirt and slid the tiny square of paper into the inside pocket where he put the tiny glasses. "—sentenced to serve life in prison in the State Prison at Cody, Wyoming."

There were gasps and moans behind me and I heard Pearline start to cry. Billy put his hand on my shoulder and I hardly knew about any of it. All I knew was what I was looking at and that was Judge Dewey, who looked straight on back at me while he buttoned his coat up tight and got up from the chair.

I'd'a given a bunch a million dollars to know what was on that tiny fold of paper, but then I decided I could save all that money I didn't really have. I knew full well what was on that sheet of paper. I knew full well.

XII

I been behind bars before, usually drunk and dumb, taking a swing at an even sloppier drunk than I was, or grabbing the curve and butt of a lady I'd forgotten to get introduced to, so it wasn't like I didn't have any experience at getting through the experience on my side. But those times before was all short-timers and those times before I was in what anyone would call a jail.

Now I was in a prison, and that's a turtle different from a tortoise. Jail's a place you get a cot and a plate of bad beans and you can handle the ride because you can see the top of the hill. Prison for an old man is just a pre-coffin and not much more. That's a mattress with no soft place to put your rump. Doesn't matter how you twist and which way you turn; it's always going to be hard and that's what you have to take in and soak up. If you can do that, there's a little smooth place that gets created, but doing that can take more time than you got left to live because doing that means letting loose of tomorrow.

They put me in two places once I got paper-worked over. Most of the old waddies they kept inside and I was no exception. The first place I was sent to was the kitchen, which meant scrubbing with something they called soap but looked a lot like pig fat to me, but there was hot water sometimes and with winter coming, that might make it a good place to be, pig fat or not. Then, at the end of every week, when Dr. Nagle came by on Friday mornings, they'd send me to what they called the infirmary, which was really just a room with four cots that had thicker mattresses than the other cell cots had and blankets with some hopeful heft to them. There was a lot of coughing spitters there, which put me to mind of the girl killed at Honey's, but Nagel dosed them dopey and when they left, they left without an abundance of harm and howl. I could help with some of the others, the ones who'd hammered their own foot with a sledge or snapped off something in their shoulder using a pick. Not that I could take over for Doc Nagle, but the time I spent with Billy, the time I spent watching Omar try to set things right, gave me a little working experience I could put to good use. No curses, just a few feel-betters for now.

The best thing about the infirmary was the window. All barred up proper, it was still big enough to look out over the road that led through the wall and on into the yard itself. On the other side of the road you could see that same road leading away to the foothills, and past the foothills, the mountains themselves, always capped in hard harsh white. I could stand up on a stool under that window and look out there for hours and know how clean the air at the top of that hard whiteness must be, how it must feel, how it must taste. Standing looking out of that window was the wrong thing for an old man to do. But that's where I was standing when I heard it.

"Moss! You got visitors."

Assistant Warden Brock was in the doorway. He was in his forties and bone lean. Brock never had a job that wasn't tied to the prison. Just a different kinda lifer from me.

I stepped down off the stool, not getting all the way easy with what he said. There was one visiting day a month and that was ten days off. I said that to Brock.

"Professional courtesy," he said. "These two come with a special official request from Marshal Ganeel in Salt Springs. You interested in seeing them or not?"

"Interested, Boss. Interested."

Billy and Pearline were waiting in the corridor outside my cell. The other two men in my cell were young bucks, so they were outside hammering big into small. Assistant Warden Brock edged me in to the cell and slammed the door shut.

"Warden Brock, is that really the way it's got to be? I'm not going anywhere."

"Moss, you're new here. I don't know why in the hell you're getting special letters about getting visitors, but you're right about one thing. You're not going anywhere and that's why the door's closed. Ten minutes, no more." He crammed the ring of keys back in to his coat pocket, then turned and went down around the corner of the block. There was a little metal clicking sound with each step he took.

"Hey, Wilbur."

"Hey, Pearline. Hey, Billy."

"Wilbur. You look good."

"I only been here three weeks, Billy. Man can't get turned inside out in three weeks, not even here." For the first time, I noticed what they were wearing. It wasn't that cold yet for what they were wearing. "Brock's not a book learner, but sometimes he finds an acorn. Why did you get a special letter from Willard to come to see me?"

"Mr. Starett asked him," Billy said.

"How come?"

"It's part of a sort of a deal I made with Starett."

"Billy," Pearline said. "Tell it all. Tell him where we're going and what's going on in Salt Springs." Her look was on him tight and she wasn't turning loose.

"We're going to Laramie," Billy said.

"Going to Laramie for how long?"

His Adam's apple worked while he chewed on some air. "For quite a while, looks like."

I looked at Pearline. "Billy isn't the teacher there anymore," she said. "Miz Starett got all ruffled about him."

Billy shook his head. This wasn't the first time they'd been having this conversation. "It wasn't Miz Starett, Pearline."

"That's what Mr. Starett said."

"That's what he said, but I don't think what he said was the real way it happened." Billy looked at me and dove in, getting it all done with. "Starett said Miz Starett wanted her books back, all of them, and I told him I couldn't teach the school without any books, and he went right on and said they'd been in touch with a lady teacher who could arrive with all the books that was needed, enough to open the school and get all the way through the year."

"So you're out."

"Like the frosty side of the window."

"Because you talked for me at the trial."

"Got no proof. Just a buncha hunch."

"Shit on a duck, Billy. I'm sorry."

"Don't be. It's not all bad."

"What's the good part?"

Billy's grin took time getting there, but it was good to see. "When Starett first talked to me about the job, I said we ought to have a paper between us and so he wrote one out."

"That's a contract," Pearline said.

"So they got to pay you."

"That's how come me and Pearline get to go to Laramie."

"To do what?" I looked over at Pearline. I never saw a person look that happy once they got past the age of four.

"They're going to open a teachers college in Laramie. Two years. If I pass the entrance and get all the way through, I'll be able to get a teaching paper. Teach anywhere in the whole state."

"Laramie's quite a way off," I said.

Pearline moved closer to the bars. "Wilbur, we'll be back to see you as soon as we get settled in. Swear it."

"And, none of my business, but what are you going to be doing in Laramie, Pearline?" I didn't like myself one bit for asking her that question.

"There are lots of silver mines in Laramie, Wilbur. That means a lot of rich people, and rich people always need cleaning ladies. I can do that; I know I can."

I snuck a look at Billy.

"What you're thinking won't happen," Billy said. "And if it does, Pearline and me will find a way to handle whatever needs handling."

Pearline stretched her hand out between the bars, took mine in hers. "We're going to be fine, Wilbur. That's why we're here. We wanted you to know we're going to be all right and we're not just moving on out of your life. We'll be here to see you as soon as we're settled in."

"Pearline, back off of that a couple steps," Billy said. "Winter comes and the pass closes, we can't get here till the thaw."

I was just looking down at Pearline's hand on mine. I lifted my other hand and touched the top of hers as lightly as I knew how. My index finger petted the top of her hand.

"Wilbur?" she said kitten soft. "Wilbur?"

It took a time before I found my voice and managed to make any kind of sound that could get turned into a word. "I know it's dumb and I know I'm dumb as well, but every time you hold out your hand, Pearline, it hits me like a hammer inside that this might be the very last time I ever feel a woman's soft touch."

"Oh, Wilbur." Pearline reached out her hand and lifted the one I was touching till she was cupping each side of my face with one of her hands. I closed my eyes and put my hands over hers. Her hands were warm, soft as new snow, and smelled of lavender. My eyes squeezed shut and something inside me started to tear away and shred. It was part Pearline, and even more part Alma; and even more than both of them, the notion of every woman I ever touched or held or warmed in my life. More than anything, it was knowing how close sundown was and how cold the night was likely to be.

"Wilbur. Oh, Wilbur."

When I finally pulled her hands away, they were shining wet on top. Don't know where that came from. I looked over at Billy standing on the other side of the bars. His face had the young-and-old thing I saw before. His face was a map leading to hurt gully. "It's late, Billy," I said. "You and Pearline got a way to go. Sun's moving; you better move, too."

"We'll stay till the man says we need to leave."

"That time is now, Billy. That time is now." I snuffed hard, wiped my nose.

"You saved my life, pardner," he said.

"You to me, Billy. Me to you."

We all heard the metal clink of Brock coming back down the corridor. "Wilbur," said Pearline, "when we have a baby, we're going to name it after you!"

I cackled. "Lord, Pearline, no. Don't ever name a baby boy Wilbur! It's kind of a curse; you can't do that to your own flesh and blood!"

"Middle name then! Middle name!"

I tried some on for size. "Charles W. Piper. Robert W. Piper. Andrew W. Piper. Okay, yeah. You might try that. That's a thing that might work." The metal clinks said Brock was right around the corner.

Billy lifted up a hand. "Hey, Wilbur."

"Hey, Billy."

"We'll see you in the spring."

"I'll be here."

They turned and left before Brock came into view.

It wasn't more than a few minutes later when I

was back standing on the stool in the infirmary, looking out the big high window again. They were just going through the gate when I got there. Made me smile to see they were riding on Black Iodine, still a touch unaccountable, dancing left and right, neck a little arched, but still under Billy's rein and doing well.

Pearline was mounted up behind Billy, her arms wrapped tight around his waist, her own personal sash on him. She had her face pressed hard into the valley between his shoulder blades, and even from this far off, I could see the Christmas morning smile on her face. Her eyes were closed, but she wasn't sleepy.

They were out of sight when the gate shut behind them. Then they came into view a bit later when they were farther on down the road. I stayed on that stool for quite some time watching them go, the wantabe-teacher and the usetabe-whore. Wasn't too long before they were small in the distance, and not long after that, they were downright tiny.

They weren't really tiny, of course. They were big as always, big as they needed to be to get over the next rise and move on into the night.

<u>Report: Deceased</u>
<u>Prisoner Disposition</u>

To: Warden T.G. Keppler

From: Assistant Warden Brock

Re: Prisoner #2679 Moss, Wilbur

Prisoner 2679 collapsed in the kitchen
scrub area 3/10/'73. Pronounced deceased
by Dr. Nagel on his next prison tour
3/14/'73. Cause of death was brain
bleeding per Nagel.

2679 remains interred in prison cemetery
3/15/'73. Reverend Calvin Parker of Sweet
Prayer Baptist Church will hold formal
burial on his arrival these premises
post thaw.

Per instructions #2679's personals to be
shipped to:

Mr. and Mrs. William Piper
c/o Public School #2
Laramie, Wyoming

Submitted for your approval.

Sincerely,

Assistant Warden P.L. Brock